TEN AGAIN

A Novel by
Michael J. Bellito

Eloquent Books

Eloquent Books
An imprint of Strategic Book Group
P.O. Box 333
Durham, CT 06422
www.StrategicBookGroup.com

ISBN: 978-1-60911-121-2

Printed in the United States of America

Cover Design: Peggy Ann Rupp, *www.netdbs.com*

Book Design: D. Johnson, Dedicated Business Solutions, Inc.

To my wonderful wife, Joani,
with heartfelt gratitude.
Thanks for sharing life with me.

CONTENTS

TEN AGAIN

PART I
SUMMER

CHAPTER 1

"OF MONSTERS AND MARBLES"

The screen door slammed open. I exploded into the sun-tinted, green-as-grass back yard on the first morning of the first day of summer. Eternity—the true meaning of summer to a ten-year-old boy—stretching out to the distant horizon with the first day of school so far away it didn't even exist. An endless series of sun-drenched, melt-in-your-mouth Popsicle days and starlit, lightning-bug nights. A giant jar of time to capture adventure with just-down-the-block friends and seal it up forever, only to peer into it when the ache of old age needs a lift.

My brother Tommy followed close behind. He knew no other way. Two years younger, he had spent every hour of every day of his life shadowing me. We shared a small bedroom in a ranch house on a corner lot in a northwest suburb of Chicago. One closet. Side-by-side matching dressers with mirrors. A desk. Bunk beds. Me on top, the sacred privilege of the first-born. We interacted together like siblings: we yelled, cursed, fought, destroyed communal property, watched too much TV, laughed, cried, and ultimately defended each other against all outsiders.

"Hey, Mike. What're we gonna do today?"

"I dunno yet," I answered haughtily. "Let's get the stuff out of the garage, and I'll hit you some grounders. Maybe Johnny'll come over."

Johnny was our best friend, another brother in spirit. He lived across the street and two houses up, toward the highway. He was Tommy's age, had a crew cut, freckles, an infectious laugh, and an easy-going temperament. His house, however, was unique for the era. It had no parent at home during the day. Johnny's dad, like all dads, worked. But his mom also worked outside the home. Head librarian at the local library. This was unheard of. Most moms had no car; many had no driver's license. Their divine calling was to stay at home, clean house, cook meals, and keep kids in line by any and all means necessary, including some that violated the Geneva Convention. This system worked well for the most part. Adult supervision gave us the greatest gift of all. We were the last generation who were allowed to be kids.

"Let's go get Johnny," I said after watching Tommy muff six ground balls in a row.

We scooted across the street and banged on the open screen door. Johnny's face appeared. "Hi."

"Hi. C'mon out."

"Can't. Patty's not up yet."

"What? Is lard ass gonna sleep all day?"

Patty was Johnny's thirteen-year-old sister, who was ostensibly in charge of him during the day but was usually either on the phone or in the bathroom. Today of all days, the first day, the greatest day, she had chosen to stay in bed.

"She'll be up soon. C'mon in." Pushing open the door, Johnny grinned, his eyes glistening in anticipation. "I gotta show you something cool."

Tommy and I glanced at each other. This had to be good. The owner of every new toy on the market, Johnny seldom disappointed. We followed him down the short hall and into the familiar bedroom. Shelves lined with model cars, his passion, greeted us as we entered. But there on his cluttered desk, surrounded by brushes and bottles of colored paint, sat a new model. It was unlike any we'd ever seen yet instantly recognizable.

"Holy shit!"

Painted green with numerous red scars, the Frankenstein Monster stepped menacingly forward from a metallic gray tombstone.

"Where d'ja get him?"

"At Walgreens. And guess what? He's not the only one. They've got Dracula and the Wolf Man too."

This was too much. Models of the Unholy Three. How many sleepless nights had they caused us? Occasionally, our parents would allow us to stay up past our bedtimes on Saturday nights to watch the venerable "Shock Theatre," a potpourri of horror guaranteed to scare us witless. The Mummy, the Creature, the Invisible Man, and other fiends would haunt our dreams and scar our psyches. But none as often or as relentlessly as Frankenstein, Dracula, and the Wolf Man—the murderers' row of monsters.

"What are you morons doing here?" The soulless voice came from the doorway. Turning to see Patty standing in her nightgown, hair in curlers and face caked with beauty cream, we quickly forgot Frankenstein.

"Hi, Sis," said Johnny with a smirk. "Sleep well?"

"Why don't you go outside and play?" she scowled. "And take your Nancy-boy playmates with you." Stalking off to the bathroom, she added over her shoulder, "And be home for lunch on time."

Once outside, we looked up and down the serene street. Rows of elm trees cast shadows across the well-manicured lawns. "Let's go round up the guys and have a game," I said.

We ambled down the street, crossed the intersection, and headed toward Jimmy's house.

Jimmy was the skinniest, fastest, and most athletic kid on the block. His natural gifts and cocky attitude combined to make him a dangerous, accident-waiting-for-a-place-to-happen kind of kid. His favorite challenge was to run out in front of slow-moving cars to see if they could stop in time. As terrified moms, blanched with fear, slammed on their brakes and jerked to a halt, Jimmy would laugh insanely and kick up his heels. Once he jumped off a ledge of bricks on the site of a house under construction, thrusting out his tongue in crazed defiance as he landed. Blood spurted from his mouth as his nearly severed tongue wagged back and forth. A panic-stricken trip to the hospital with his hysterical mother resulted in a jagged row of stitches, which he proudly displayed to curious onlookers for years to come.

Jimmy's mom met us at the door.

"Morning, Mrs. O'Donnell. Can Jimmy come out and play?"

"Jimmy!" she screamed over her shoulder. She was famous in the neighborhood for that scream. Day or night, it pierced the solitude of our quiet street. Once when Jimmy and I were casually walking to school, we heard a shriek split the still morning air behind us. Whirling around, we saw Mrs. O'Donnell two blocks back, sporting pink robe and curlers, frantically waving something in her hand. "Jimmy! You forgot your pencils!"

"Asshole," he muttered and kept walking.

Another time, Tommy and I were waiting outside for our friends to come by before school when we saw Jimmy's older sister get on the high school bus. As the bus began to pull away, Mrs. O'Donnell threw herself in front of it and pounded on the door. "Stop! Stop!" Stepping on, she faced a sullen, shocked-into-silence mass of teens. "Kelley!" came the high-pitched wail-from-beyond-the-grave. "Shame on you! You forgot your lunch! It's your favorite, egg salad sandwich and Fritos!" We were told that Kelley cried all the way to school.

"Jimmy!" she yelled even louder. "Can't you hear me? The boys are here to play!"

Jimmy never walked anywhere. Before Mrs. O'Donnell knew he was there, he had shot past us onto the dew-covered front lawn, his arms waving as he sang aloud, "It's sum- sum- sum- sum- summertime!"

Laughing, we scrambled after him. Mrs. O'Donnell's last minute, frantic instructions followed us down the street, to be devoutly ignored. "Boys! Don't-play-rough, don't-climb-trees, don't-run-in-the-street, look-both-ways! Boys! Do you hear me?"

A blue jay, squawking in distress, burst from the upper branches of a nearby tree.

The next stop on the block was Eddie's house, where he and Greg were engaged in a duel-to-the-death match of marbles on a patch of dirt by the driveway.

"Hey," I said in greeting. "Let's get some more guys and play ball!"

"In a minute," came Eddie's terse reply. "I'm trying to win back my cat's-eye."

Whoa. This was serious business. We stared in silent suspense as Eddie leaned forward on his hands and knees, carefully calculating his shot. He took a deep breath and held it. Click.

"Yes," he exhaled, pumping a triumphant fist into the air. "It's mine again."

"Lucky shot," groused Greg.

Eddie grabbed the clear, green-streaked marble and thrust it back into its leather pouch. His pudgy arm reached up and wiped the glistening beads of sweat off his forehead. With a sigh of relief, he looked up at us as if seeing us for the first time. "So, what're you boys up to?"

Eddie was short and plump, making him the butt of all the fat jokes in the neighborhood. Bright-eyed and amiable, he never seemed to mind the teasing. His innate politeness came from having been raised in the South for the first eight years of his life. He always addressed adults, including his own parents, "sir" or "ma'am," a custom that baffled his newly found friends. The most likely explanation for his manners was his strict upbringing. I had once witnessed Eddie's father whipping him with a belt in broad daylight behind the garage as punishment for some transgression. No wonder he was always home on time for dinner.

Greg, on the other hand, had no father. A taciturn boy, he was being raised by his widowed mother after his father, a newspaperman, had died of a sudden heart attack. Greg's mom was the only single parent on the block, divorce being uncommon in those days. Eager to please, Greg loved being included in our games; because he was a born athlete, we were glad to have him.

Our number now six, we could have played a variety of street games, but we had outgrown those the past summer. I forcefully rallied the troops. "Listen up. Eddie, you and Greg go across the street and get Denny. Jimmy, you cut through the back yard and get Bobby."

We all loved Denny. His dad had the coolest job on the block. A cop. And not an ordinary cop either. A state trooper. When he cruised down our street in his Illinois State Police car, heads always turned. If we were playing catch on someone's front lawn, we'd gesture with a circular motion at him. He'd smile and oblige by turning on the siren. Denny was a lot like his dad. Tall and sinewy with a dark complexion, always flashing a bright-white smile. Not arrogant, but sure of himself. Someone who was going to be somebody.

Bobby, like Eddie, had been brought up elsewhere, near Philadelphia. He had actually moved into the neighborhood three years earlier, but it took us awhile to get to know him because he lived on the next street over—a separate planet in those days.

"Make sure everybody brings their gloves 'cause we're gonna play hardball," I ordered. "We'll meet back here at ten o'clock sharp and head for the field. Bring your bikes."

Bikes. A magic word for us. Bikes meant freedom. Freedom to go anywhere—the ball field, the swimming pool, the movie theatre, the little store. The latter was found in every suburb in America during its heyday. Called mom-and-pop stores, they were family owned and operated. Run by immigrants from various ethnic tribes, they carried almost every item found in larger grocery stores. Canned soups and vegetables, cold and

hot cereals, pastas, soapsuds, and a multitude of household cleaning supplies. Ours, overseen by Mr. and Mrs. Garheimer, was called the little store because—well, because it wasn't big. We relished our trips there to buy candy (penny, two-penny, and nickel variety), ten-cent ice cream bars from the big glass freezer, and five-cent packs of baseball cards. However, the privilege of owning a bike carried with it the responsibility of running errands to the little store to pick up milk, bread, and other necessities from time to time.

My bike that summer was a brand new, red and silver 26-inch Schwinn Traveler, named after Confederate General Robert E. Lee's magnificent horse, or so I claimed. It had exactly one speed—as slow or as fast as I pedaled—foot brakes, and ugly metal baskets on each side of the rear wheel, a concession to my parents upon its purchase for those little store runs. To detract from the hideous baskets, I immediately decorated it with cool sports stickers (Cubs, Sox, Bears, Fighting Irish). These, along with the sleek power of the block's biggest bike, gave me a proud-as-a-parent attitude whenever I rode, condescending to the other kids to ride alongside them.

Our bikes, a variety of shapes, sizes, and colors, hurtled helter-skelter toward the ball field. The whooping, shrieking boys upon them carried favorite bats, balls, and gloves, the scuffed leather and wood "autographed" by Hank Aaron, Mickey Mantle, and other stars of the day. We pedaled furiously, and I felt in my heart what I could not have known—that life would never again be such fast-paced, frenetic fun. As our tires screamed across the hot pavement, the summer sun beat down on our heads, holding us in its viselike grip.

Chapter 2
"Play Ball!"

The freshly mowed expanse of green beckoned to us as we approached the end of the block. Here, our street formed a "t" with another, the symbolic gateway to our personal heaven. The field was a lush area of fertile soil and turf adjacent to the Old People's Home. No diamond of dirt was marked upon it; no backstop glistened in the bright morning light.

"Set up the bases!" I yelled as soon as our bikes hit the ground. The bases could be anything—caps, sticks, towels, cardboard—but were most often Frisbees brought from home.

"Choose up sides," said Jimmy.

"Gotta pick captains first," Denny reminded us.

"Put in your feet," I commanded.

Our right feet met in a circle.

"Blue shoe, blue shoe, how old are you?" I intoned, stabbing with my forefinger at each tennis shoe in turn.

The quick count. The sudden elimination. Only Eddie and I remained. Alternating picks, I ended up with Bobby, Tommy, and Greg while Eddie claimed Johnny, Jimmy, and Denny. Fair sides. A good balance.

"All right," I said. "Listen up. Everybody plays pitcher, shortstop, and two outfielders. Catch for your own team when you're up to bat. Pitcher's hands out. Anything hit to the right of second base is an automatic out, except when Bobby's up. Then you guys gotta switch fields."

Eddie's entire team groaned in unison. With my first pick, I had chosen Bobby, the only lefty among us, thus condemning the other team to a constant game of diamond roulette whenever they were in the field.

"We get last ups," I threw in quickly, knowing I had violated an unwritten code.

"No way!" yelled Eddie. "You had first dibs. We get last ups."

"He's right, Mike," chimed in Jimmy.

"Of course he's right, Einstein," I said, embarrassed they had caught me. "Everybody knows that. I just wanted to see if he was paying attention. Let's play ball!"

That we would have played anything other than baseball was tantamount to heresy. This was 1960, after all, and baseball was still king, the undisputed national pastime. Kids played baseball on grass fields, dirt diamonds, concrete streets, asphalt driveways; they played slow pitch, fast pitch, underhand, overhand, softball, hardball, even wiffleball. The latter provided hours of intense fun for as few as two players. With the small, plastic ball, one could throw change-ups, wicked curves, and even the dreaded knuckleball. Plus, wiffleball games could be played under the glaring beam of the garage lights, creating the ambiance of real night baseball.

In those days, the Major Leagues were comprised of a mere sixteen teams, two of which resided in Chicago. Since WGN-TV televised the Cubs and White Sox, both of whom were championed by the ebullient Jack Brickhouse, most suburban kids didn't favor one or the other. It was, of course, easy to cheer for the winning White Sox, who had brought an A.L. pennant to the city the previous fall, their first since they had conspired with gamblers to throw the 1919 World Series. Led by exciting players such as Luis Aparicio, Nellie Fox, and Jim Landis, the Sox were especially embraced by Mayor Richard J. Daley, who set off the city's air-raid sirens on the night of the pennant-clinching victory. The panic-stricken reaction—elderly citizens stumbling down stairways in search of bomb shelters—didn't seem to bother the overjoyed South Sider.

The Cubs, on the other hand, lost year after year while drawing increasingly smaller crowds to Wrigley Field.

But every kid in Chicagoland loved Ernie Banks, the star shortstop—the word "superstar" had not yet been invented—who hit home runs, won back-to-back MVP awards, and, every spring, cheerfully predicted a glorious rise from the depths of baseball hell for his beloved Cubs.

Regardless of one's leanings, kids growing up in and around Chicago were able, in the days before Interleague play, to see all the N.L. and A.L. visiting stars, a unique privilege. And we knew the names and positions of all the Major Leaguers too, mostly thanks to baseball cards.

Baseball cards. Was there ever a greater product than those gum-scented, sticky-smooth pieces of cardboard that sold at the little store for five cents a pack? Included with five cards was a slim piece of pink bubble gum, saved for game days when we would shove stacks into our mouths to emulate Pirate second baseman Bill Mazeroski's plug of chewing tobacco. The cards were gathered sporadically throughout the long summer, organized into teams, and held together with rubber bands. Team cards were placed on top, manager cards came next, then stars, regulars, and finally all the pitchers, starters on top of relievers. On any rainy day, I would set up a makeshift diamond on my bedroom rug, bases and pitcher's mound cut from paper, and play elaborately devised games with the cards.

Shuffling through the familiar faces, I rapidly selected the day's starting line-ups for each team. Following a scratchy phonograph rendition of "The Star Spangled Banner," the home team, usually the White Sox or Cubs, took the field, and nine innings of the greatest baseball game ever created in a kid's imagination began. An old twelve-number spinner from a Howdy Doody board game determined, through an intricate series of spins, the strikes, balls, ground outs, fly outs, walks, errors, singles, doubles, triples, and homers. Even double plays occurred, although probably not as often as real Cub batters bounced into them.

I, of course, managed both teams, deftly substituting pinch hitters and relief pitchers into the contest at the appropriate times. Occasionally, I would slowly slide a card along the rug as Casey Stengel or Al Lopez strolled to the mound to calm a rattled pitcher's nerves. A simple nod to the bullpen meant a trip to the showers for Whitey Ford or Early Wynn.

As if that wasn't enough power, I also announced the game. "There's a long drive into deep left-center field! Nobody's going to get this one! Landis will chase it down as it bounces off the bricks, but not before Mantle scores easily from second on a stand-up double for Berra! And that ties the game at three apiece here in the top of the sixth!" Players' cards were moved simultaneously, imitating the action of a real game. I ignored the obvious, that Mickey and Yogi carried their bats with them around the bases.

Meanwhile, majestically overlooking center field, the granddaddy of all props stood, a giant Hamm's beer scoreboard that my father had surprised me with one day. Within its cavernous structure, it held two pinwheels, each listing the names of all sixteen Major League teams. The visiting (top) and home (bottom) teams could, with the spin of a finger, be moved into place. Teams could score up to nine runs in each half inning, and the "TO-TAL" scores at the end went up to thirty-nine, in case the Yankees came to town. In the middle of the big blue board was the Hamm's Bear, wearing a generic baseball uniform and socking one out of the park. The ad read: "Watch Cubs and Sox baseball on WGN-TV brought to you by Hamm's the beer refreshing!"

If there was any problem with the indoor league, it was the missing players. Although I officially placed them on the "Disabled List," they were, in reality, MIAs. I didn't have their cards. Because Topps released its sets in seven separate series during the spring and summer, once a series was off the market, the only way to get a missing card was to trade with friends.

I traded most often with Bobby. Sitting on the back steps of my house, I sifted eagerly through his "doubles" pile. "Got 'im, got 'im, got 'im, need 'im," I smiled, pausing to set a card aside. The "got 'im, need 'im" chant continued repetitively until a small stack of Bobby's cards waited patiently for the bartering to begin. Bobby slowly flipped through my "doubles," placing aside a few. The trading itself was over in five efficient minutes. Time to pack up.

"Wait," said Bobby in a halting voice, and I knew what was coming. "You still got that Eddie Bouchee card?"

"No," I replied. "I sold it to the Russians."

Bobby was a die-hard Phillies fan, and every year it was the same thing. He would trade stars like Kaline and Killebrew to get any Phillies players.

"I really need it. I'll make you a good deal."

What happened next defied all logic. Bobby slowly reached into his pocket and pulled out four Cub pitchers: Moe Drabowsky, Glen Hobbie, Dave Hillman, and Don Elston. The drool slid slowly out of my mouth and down my chin.

"You're kiddin', right?"

"No. I gotta have Bouchee."

I reached into the shoebox at my side, pulled out the Phillies team, snapped off the rubber band, and slipped out the first baseman's card. "I've already got Elston. But I'll take the other three."

"Deal," murmured Bobby softly, and as I handed over his Holy Grail, I saw tears well up in the corners of his eyes.

On our ball field, the game was in the seventh inning with Eddie's team leading 8-6 when the noon whistle sounded. Provided free-of-charge for the downtown workers, the blaring horn was also the universal signal for summertime fun to take a break.

"We'll finish after lunch!" I shouted, scooping up my bat and glove and heading for my bike. The midday interruption meant nothing to us; we would resume our game by one or two o'clock, double- and triple-headers being as common as earthworms after rain. And if, by chance, Bobby had a dentist appointment or Jimmy was grounded for throwing food at the table, then one of us would volunteer to be "all-time pitcher," and the game, like life itself, would go on, boys hollering and arguing and laughing in the scorching summer sun.

Occasionally, we would meet after dinner for a quick game as dusk slid softly toward darkness. Such was our desire to play on that first evening of summer.

"Home run!" screamed Jimmy.

"Foul ball!" yelled Bobby, refusing to chase down the bounding ball as Jimmy danced deliriously around the base path.

"Look where it is, moron!" I implored, joining the fray.

"It's not where it is now, dick head!" shot back Jimmy, the veins in his neck bulging out. "It's where it landed! Game over! We win!"

I stood on the pitcher's rubber, a broken slat of wood, and watched Jimmy, surrounded by his joyful teammates, jumping up and down on the orange Frisbee that was home plate. I glanced toward left field where Bobby was sitting cross-legged in the grass, head down, pouting. I heaved a Charlie Brown sigh, conceding defeat, and trudged dejectedly to the sidelines.

The next half hour was spent lying on our backs, staring at the sky, the summer's many possibilities pinballing around in our heads.

" . . . and my dad says we can drive up to Milwaukee to see the Braves play sometime," I dreamed aloud.

"Impossible," argued Denny. "Milwaukee's a billion miles away."

"That's a lie," piped up Johnny, whose family spent two weeks in August every year on Washington Island in

Door County, the thumb of Wisconsin's hand. "We drive through it every summer. It's not that far."

During a lull in the dream weaving, Jimmy sat up suddenly, staring in the direction of the Old People's Home. The glint in his eyes spoke passionately of a brand new adventure. "Hey, men, I know what we can do. Unless you're chicken."

We all sat up in turn.

"Well, we're not sneakin' around Elmer's, that's for sure," said Eddie, clearly frightened.

Elmer's farm sat just beyond the nursing home and was well known in neighborhood legend. Many were the tales of terror passed down to younger generations regarding its eccentric owner. Elmer supposedly hated everyone but was particularly venomous when it came to children. He jealously guarded every square foot of his property, and if some wayward boy attempted to cut through his cornfield, a double-barreled shotgun awaited him.

"Eddie's right," I stated firmly. "He'll kill us all."

"I'm not talking about Elmer's," said Jimmy. "I'm talking about that." His slender finger pointed in the direction of the nearly completed addition to the Old People's Home.

With the construction workers gone for the day, the empty shell beckoned us like lemmings toward its twisting maze of concrete corridors, spiral staircases, and hidden rooms, the ideal setting for a raucous game of hide-and-seek. That the obvious dangers that awaited us were more real than the phantom farmer never occurred to us.

It was, in the end, wild-child Jimmy who stepped on the rusty nail, driving it painfully into the sole of his foot. He had been "it" and was in the act of running in and out of second floor rooms searching for the rest of us, who were tucked out-of-sight in corners and crevices. His screams startled us out of our hidden lairs. Horrified, we watched our friend writhing on the floor, chalky dust covering his T-shirt and shorts.

"Help me," he begged, but in the end only Jimmy was brave enough to pull the bent piece of metal out of his own foot. Reluctantly, he tugged off his tennis shoe and sock and turned his foot over. A shaft of sinking sunlight streaming through a nearby doorway illuminated what we would rather not have seen. Blood seeped from a medium-sized hole near his big toe. Placing his fingers around the wound, he squeezed hard once, making the blood run faster.

"Oh, man, you're screwed," I said.

"It'll be okay," he said stoically. "It doesn't even hurt that much."

"No," I continued, "that's not what I meant. You're going to have to get a tetanus shot."

The mere mention of it sent a shudder around our circle. Although it was quickly determined that none of us had ever had one, we readily voiced our opinions about it.

"The needle's real long."

"They stick it right in your stomach."

"It hurts for days, like cramps."

"Sometimes it doesn't work, and your foot turns green and falls off."

"Or you die."

"Shut up!" I yelled. "Can't you see you're not helping? C'mon, Jimmy. We'll get you home and tell your mom. Do you think you can walk on it?"

And so the first day, the best day, ended with one of life's many lessons. It was not to be the last time one of us embarked on a dangerous or foolish adventure. However, we never did play in that particular building again. As for Jimmy, he didn't die. In fact, he was running out in front of cars again within a week. He was, after all, just a kid.

Chapter 3

"Water World"

Tommy, Johnny, and I shot past the ancient, red brick high school, the chill morning breeze slapping our arms and faces as we rode. We turned onto the tree-lined avenue where the most well-kept, luxurious houses stood. Riding on the sidewalk, we approached a row of bushes, reached out our left hands without losing speed, and each grabbed a handful of dark green leaves. For these were no ordinary leaves. These were "lucky leaves."

The mystical name had been bestowed on them by the three of us a year earlier. We had been then, as we were now, pedaling to the town's municipal pool for swimming lessons on a particularly cold morning. In desperation, I had snatched the leaves, ridden a few blocks more, tossed them up in the air, and chanted, "Let the water be warm!" Magically, the pool's unheated water, which was usually North Atlantic cold, was not even a bit frigid that day. When Tommy and Johnny joined me in the ritual the next day, and the water was again mild, we knew divine intervention was at hand. Thus, the urban myth of the "lucky leaves" was born.

Sliding our bikes into the racks, we hurried into the old building and down the steps into the boys' locker room. Quick change into trunks. Required shower—was this really necessary? Out through the tunnel into the morning light to gather with other shivering, blue-lipped children near the edge of the pool. We were "intermediates," beyond learning to swim but another year away from the deep end and its intimidating diving boards. By summer's end, however, we would be required to dive off the low boards. If we had known this then, we probably would have run off to Texas.

"All right! Grab your paddle boards and give me twenty laps!" shouted Michelle, our instructor. With blond hair and blue eyes, she was the vixen of our daydreams. Truth be told, we would have swum the English Channel if she had commanded us to do so. Like deranged water buffalo, the herd of children jumped in, a cacophony shattering the morning silence.

The water was warmer than the air. Protected from the wind, kicking madly across the width of the pool, I breathed a prayer of thanks to the "lucky leaves." After warm-ups, we practiced various strokes. "Today we'll work on our breaststrokes," said Michelle, and Tommy giggled until snot came out of his nose.

We loved swimming so much that hot afternoons often found us scurrying back to spend countless hours in the water. This was, of course, a full hour after we had finished our peanut butter and jelly or bologna sandwiches. Every mom in the world was aware of the unwritten "eat-swim-die" rule, and they were not embarrassed about holding up kids who flagrantly disobeyed it as "foolish" and "irresponsible."

Unlike the morning hours, the pool now teemed with a tide of color and motion. Kids screamed, shouted, and splashed in the bright blue water, a mad swirl of pre-pubescent energy. On the sidelines, bronzed, bikini-clad beauties lay stretched out on a rainbow of colored towels, teasing teenage boys who wore Elvis haircuts. In the deep end, a tanned Adonis came hurtling off the high dive and down from the sky, his "cannonball" sending a volcanic-like eruption of water jetting upward to a worshipful chorus of "oohs" and "aahs" from the stunned spectators.

Overseeing the madness in slow motion were our modern-day saviors, the lifeguards. They posed in a seemingly casual manner, one sun-drenched leg draped over the side of their chairs, with white cream smeared across their faces and dark glasses reflecting the sun's metallic rays. But let just one stupid kid display running-along-poolside-jumping-on-top-of-others-diving-in-the-shallow-end behavior, and the guard would bolt to life. The silver whistle would spring into action like Wyatt Earp's Buntline Special. The ear-piercing shriek would freeze the entire pool as everyone spun around to see what reckless action was taking place. Clearly, someone had violated one of the 2,483 pool rules, all posted on giant signs along the chain-link fences. Most often, the transgressor was given a warning with a clear message: "One more time, kid, and you're outta here!"

Seldom did anyone actually get kicked out for running, jumping, or diving infractions, but sometimes boys were removed for holding little kids' heads underwater until they choked or whipping down their friends' trunks in front of the high school girls. Typical childish behavior, beneath my dignity.

For the most part, we whiled away the days practicing our strokes, playing tag games among groups of chatting children, and seeing how long we could hold our breaths underwater. The latter was accomplished by standing in one spot or by attempting to swim the width of the pool, our noses scraping along the rough bottom. No matter what the record time was, somebody always had to break it. Much lying ensued.

"Forty-four, forty-five, forty-six . . . that's forty-six seconds, a new record!" yelled Tommy as I exploded out of the water gasping for air.

"That's nothing," said Johnny. "When I was here last week, I was under for fifty-three seconds!"

"What?" I asked incredulously. "When were you here without us? And besides, I once stayed under for a whole minute!"

Before the back-and-forth was over, one of us had held his breath for nine hours and fifteen minutes.

Practicing our strokes had two purposes, one worthwhile, the other self-serving. The first was to continue to learn what we had been taught. The second was to attract the attention of Michelle, who was perched goddess-like high above us on her throne. "Michelle!" I shouted above the din. "Watch this!" I performed a flawless backstroke past her post, smiling stupidly up into her silhouette.

Her angelic voice floated down from the heavens. "That's very good, Mike!"

"Watch this, Michelle!" yelled Tommy, not to be out-done.

Our limited repertoire was burned out in minutes, and Michelle, I'm sure, turned her thoughts to other possible beaus, leaving us to amuse each other by farting under-water and watching the bubbles burst on the surface.

Another infrequent pastime was to challenge each other to see who was brave enough to jump—not dive—off the low boards into the deep end. This always ended in a stalemate, bravado taking a back seat to sanity, until one day Jimmy came with us to the pool. We dared him and then watched in horrified amazement as he calmly walked to the board, got on it, and suddenly sprinted for-ward at full speed. Reaching the end, he threw himself carelessly out into open air, yelling Tarzan-like as his little body cascaded downward, hitting the water with a joyous splash. We froze, our feet rooted to the concrete, and waited for Jimmy to reappear. We feared he never would.

As seconds ticked by, we saw his silent form shoot up from the depths. Like a flying fish, he broke the water's surface, directing a goofy grin in our direction. He swam to the side and pulled himself out of the pool. "See," he stated. "Nothing to it."

We were utterly ashamed. If Jimmy could do it, why couldn't we? Well, for one thing, we argued, Jimmy was infamous for daredevil stunts that landed him in the hos-pital with broken bones, dislocated joints, and innumer-able lacerations. It was probably mere luck that he hadn't tripped and knocked out his front teeth or landed wrong in the water and severed his spinal cord. Who were we to tempt fate?

That having been considered, we all took turns that day shoring up our courage and eventually making the jump. Once accomplished, it quickly became just another commonplace activity, like riding our bikes "no hands" or climbing to the top of the weeping willow in the back yard. The high dive, stark and terrifying, still loomed above us, however. A daily reminder of dragons yet to slay.

The park district's pool was not its only lure. There was the once-in-a-lifetime possibility of spying on naked women as they changed in the girls' locker room. All one had to do was post a lookout, climb over a short wire fence, creep through pristine flower beds, and crawl behind giant evergreen bushes. Behind the bushes, blocked from a casual observer's view, were the tops of basement windows. There, nestled out of sight in the cool shade, a boy would lie on his stomach in the moist dirt and peek downward through the slats of the shuttered windows. If he was caught slithering out of his hedonistic heaven by an angry adult, he could always lie.

"I was chasing a rabbit, and he went back in there."

"I wanted to pick some flowers for my mother."

"I had to take a leak real bad, mister!"

But the absolute cure for this type of errant behavior was the random chance of seeing one's own mom in the buff, a sight that would most likely scare one into a lifetime of celibacy. So, although we were aware of the sacred spot, we never actually risked it. Well, maybe once.

Unlike the thrills of swimming and spying, Tommy and I condescended once a week to attend "craft corner." This was a bogus park district money-making machine that parents loved. Ours signed us up with the hope that we would one day become the next Picasso or Van Gogh or maybe Betsy Ross. While there, we were encouraged to be artistic, creative, sensitive to beauty, and other attributes alien to our dirt-under-the-nails personalities.

"Today," said Betty, our cherubic counselor, "we are going to sew pillows for our moms. Won't that be fun?"

Yeah, I thought, like having hot tar poured into my nostrils.

"This is what your pillow will look like when it's finished," she said, holding aloft a perfectly plump specimen. "These, children, are the materials you will use to complete the project."

I gasped aloud when she held up a sewing needle the size of a small spear. All the girls giggled excitedly. Couldn't anyone see the sexism here? Needless to say, my brother and I did not create anything even closely resembling the prototype. In fact, Tommy broke down crying halfway through while I gamely finished my wretched excuse for a pillow, stabbing myself repeatedly in the process. I held it up to show Betty, blood slowly trickling down my palm.

"That's nice, Mike," she said. "I'm sure your mother will love it."

Of course, she'll love it, you idiot. She's my mother. But if I show it to the kids on the block, they'll stone me to death.

"Oh, everyone! Look at Laura's! Isn't it beautiful?"

I scraped my little brother off the dirt beneath the picnic table, and we shuffled home.

My head hurt. My muscles ached. But most of all, my left arm, swollen from a triple booster shot the day before, radiated intense pain. Miserable, I lay on the couch on a gorgeous Sunday afternoon in June watching the Yankees beat the life out of the White Sox in a doubleheader. In those days, it was common for kids to get shots for every childhood disease known to man. But I could never remember one ruining a summer's day with such a violent reaction. And to top it off, Tommy and Johnny had gone to the pool without me, leaving me alone in the darkened living room.

Suddenly, the back door crashed open, and I heard the traitors walking rapidly across the kitchen floor toward my den of sorrow.

"Hey, Mike," said Johnny, "how're you feelin'?"

"Sick," I answered feebly.

The two sat down on chairs opposite me. They stole apprehensive glances at one another until they could hold it in no longer.

"Tell him," said Tommy.

"Oh, no. He's your brother. You tell him."

After a long pause, Tommy fixed his eyes on my sunken frame. "Now, don't get mad." Another long pause. "We both went off the high dive today."

I groaned. I wanted to leap up from my sick bed and call them liars, but I knew in my heart that they spoke the truth. My little brother and his even littler friend had accomplished the unthinkable while I lay dying. The contrast was clear: their strength versus my weakness, their courage versus my cowardice, their heroics versus my frailties. I was doomed. Destined to lie weakly on the couch forever, the outside world closed off by the drawn drapes, while Tommy and Johnny conquered new horizons without me.

"We're sorry," said Johnny. "But you can jump off it later this week when you're feeling well again."

"Yeah," encouraged Tommy. "It's easy. You'll see."

And he was right. True friends might do something stupid once in a while, but they'd stand by you when you really needed them. They were both beside me three days later, cheering me on, when I walked bravely to the ladder, climbed it, stepped tentatively to the edge of the board, peeked off the side of the earth, and jumped wide-eyed into the crystal blue water below.

CHAPTER 4

"GOD BLESS AMERICA"

I awoke to the sound of my father's voice filtering back through the house from the kitchen. Why was Dad home from work? And then it hit me. Today was the best day of mid-summer. Parade, picnic, and fireworks all lay ahead like an unbroken series of presents. I bolted out of bed shouting, "Tommy, get up! It's the Fourth of July!"

Our town had a history of doing it right. The parade was a tradition dating back through the decades, and everyone was either in it or came to watch it. There were: the Boy and Girl Scouts, ancient flivvers, fire trucks, acrobats, clowns, bikes, bands, and floats. Never in our young lives had we been privileged to ride on one of the elaborately decorated flatbeds, but that was to change this year. Johnny's mother had helped design the library's entrée, and she had consented to allow Johnny and two of his friends—who else?—to sit on the back and pitch penny candy to children. We were ecstatic.

As we shoveled down bowls of Cocoa Krispies, Tommy and I chattered excitedly about the upcoming honor. "Think about it," I mumbled through a mouthful. "We'll be famous all over town. Jimmy and Bobby will go nuts when they see us."

"Yeah, and we can give 'em the finger when we go by," laughed Tommy, snorting milk out of his nose.

"You'll do no such thing!" Our mother had been cleaning up our little sister Linda's face, which was covered with Cheerios. She glared icily at us, her eyes slits of glass. "Now you listen and you listen well." Gesturing with the cereal-coated dishcloth, she continued. "This is a wonderful opportunity for you two to make a good impression on this community, and I will not have you embarrassing this family with your hijinks. You will sit like little angels, if such a thing is possible, and wave politely to the crowd. You will not, at any time, stand up, run, jump, or try to push each other off the float."

A really cool idea burst into my brain and was censored just as suddenly.

"Do I make myself clear?"

We nodded.

"Good. Because if I get so much as one bad word from Mrs. Ellison about your behavior, neither of you will be able to sit down for a week. Now, finish your breakfast and go get dressed. I set out your outfits on your beds."

Outfits—a good word for them; they certainly weren't normal clothes like other boys wore. Our mother had long been under the delusion that Tommy and I were twins. Why else the demented desire to dress us exactly alike for every holiday or special occasion? Today's costumes were, fittingly, red and white vertically striped shirts, navy blue shorts, white socks, and blue tennis shoes with white laces. My country 'tis of thee . . .

"Oh, no," Tommy wailed. "This is crap. We're gonna look like the flag."

"We're gonna look worse than that. Just shut up and get dressed, okay?"

A half hour later, Dad dropped us off on the other side of the railroad tracks, where the parade was gradually falling into place. Park district organizers, almost all women, were bustling about, blubbery arms waving frantically, shouting into megaphones that crackled with commands. These perennial Pattons were clearly in their element, relishing every moment of glory as floats, horses, bands, and banners were all slid neatly into their assigned slots like a thousand-piece jigsaw puzzle in the hands of a gifted grandma.

"No! No! Not there!" yelled one stout woman wearing an Uncle Sam hat and a bright red dress covered with stars. "It's Brownie Troop 437, then the unicycles!"

Zigzagging through the maze, my brother and I finally found the library float. It didn't look half bad. A papier-mâché brick building rose from a grass-colored base with several trees surrounding it. Hanging from the tree limbs was an assortment of giant-sized books, white-letter titles such as *Tom Sawyer* and *The Cat in the Hat* standing out against the dark covers. A huge sign stating—predictably, I thought—READ! was suspended over the top of the float. Johnny, dressed normally, stood looking up at the beast.

"We're here," I said as we approached.

"Ha. Nice duds. Are you boys ready to roll?"

We were. Johnny handed us bags of candy, individually wrapped pieces of caramel, licorice, and flavored taffy. "My mom says not to get carried away and use it all up at the beginning. It's a long parade."

Long, indeed. And hot. The temperature was to soar into the nineties by mid-afternoon, and now, at eight-thirty in the morning, it was already sticky. Promptly at nine o'clock—the ladies would have it no other way—the parade kicked off. Across the tracks. Through downtown. Up shady avenues. Toward the community park. Bystanders lined the route, children hunched on curbs, old people sunk into lawn chairs. Everyone clapped and cheered and waved miniature flags and came together as one to celebrate all that was good about our still-young country.

And contrary to urban legend, Tommy and I behaved for once. It's true that a misguided missile of hard candy struck a small child in the eye. But since neither of us could throw that accurately, it was put down as an unfortunate accident. We did see Jimmy and Bobby with their folks, but we wisely refrained from saluting them. All in all, our venture out into the public eye was, I thought, a success. God bless America.

An hour after the parade lurched to an untimely halt when the fire truck broke down a block from the park, we were nestled into the old Buick along with some pop and potato salad, off to join other families for a traditional picnic. Because we only saw these four or five clans once a year, an awkward period of re-acquaintance always preceded the genuine fun we had at the farm-like house in the country. Kids played softball on the freshly mowed lawn. Moms set out an assortment of homemade recipes, from baked beans to pickled cucumbers to German potato salad to a variety of cakes and fruit pies. Dads drank beer, played horseshoes, and shared World War II hyperboles until the moms called on them to charcoal-grill the burgers and franks, where they drank more beer in the process.

For the next hour, laughter rang like church bells across the burning fields as, huddled beneath the shade of an old oak tree, we listened in awe to amazing anecdotes from when our parents were kids. When the last crumb of apple pie was gone, washed down with a slug of cream soda, one of the moms said, "Why don't you kids go play some more? We'll cut the watermelon later."

So off we went, ranging in ages from two to sixteen, the big ones always keeping an eye out for the little ones. We chased Frisbees, knocked croquet balls about, and played tag. The sizzling summer sun buzzed above us.

"Mikey, come here!"

I broke from a game of crack the whip and ran to my father. Weighing in at roughly 260 lbs., dressed in an untucked plaid shirt and tan slacks, he was a formidable figure. He held a cold can of beer in one hand, a cigar in the other, and wore an Indian chief's war bonnet atop his bald head. He was smiling. "I got something here, but it's only for the big kids. You understand?"

He set down his sweat-soaked can and reached behind the drink table, producing a brown paper bag.

Peering inside, I saw the thin cardboard boxes painted red, white, and blue that could mean only one thing. "Yes," I said. "Sparklers!"

"Now, remember, these are not for the little kids. Keep them away when you light them. Here are some matches."

I scooted across the yard, cut the older kids from the mix, and we wandered back behind the old barn where the property line nudged up against a barren field of wild grass. The great thing about sparklers was that they looked cool in the daytime as well as at night. As soon as someone held a match to the tip of one, it burst into noisy, vibrant light, white sparks flying out in every direction. Holding them at arm's length for fear of being set on fire, we twirled them in circles and wrote our names in the air.

"Watch this!" I yelled. Just before my sparkler burned out, I bent my knees, sprang upward, and tossed it high into the air. Framed against the blue-gray sky, it carried ten yards or so of open space and plummeted into the high grass, landing out of sight.

One of the teenagers, Allen, glared harshly at me. "You idiot! Go get that! It could start a fire!"

Oh, my Lord. I'd never thought of that. A hot, windy day; a dry field; a careless act.

As I stumbled into the bug-infested, waist-high weeds, my panic-stricken brain visualized the impending catastrophe. Black smoke curling up out of the prairie grass ahead of me. A blast of red-orange flame. The whipping wind. The blaze gaining momentum and propelling itself toward the horizon. Me standing stiffly, crying terrified tears as the raging inferno consumed everything in its path. Houses. Barns. Livestock. People. Days later, reduced to glowing embers, it would be compared to the Great Chicago Fire in lives lost and property destroyed. Newspaper headlines would scream: STUPID TEN-YEAR-OLD PLAYS WITH SPARKLERS, BURNS COUNTRYSIDE.

Sweat streamed down my face. Sharp brambles scraped my bare legs. Intoning whispered prayers, I searched from side to side for the grounded missile. A giant dragonfly darted past my field of vision, fleeing the imminent conflagration.

Suddenly, a stick-shaped object showed itself, wedged in the brown grass below. Swooping down like a bomber pilot, I reached my hand out and clutched it. Thank the Saints, it was the sparkler. The still red-hot end of the sparkler.

"Aaaaaah!" I stared at the palm of my hand. An ugly red welt stared back. I fled the field past the stunned group of guys who weren't sure what had happened. A bee sting? A jagged piece of glass? I ran all the way to the comforting arms of my mom, her lemon chiffon dress a beacon in the distance. She heard me coming.

"What happened, sweetheart?"

I showed her the swollen streak.

"Oh, Mikey. What did you do?"

"I burned it. On a sparkler."

"A sparkler! Where on earth did you get a sparkler?"

"It hurts," I cried, refusing to give up my dad under coercion.

"Oh, we've got to get some butter on that right away," she said, alluding to an old-fashioned, ridiculous remedy for treating burns.

For the remainder of that afternoon, I sat slumped in a wicker chair, my greasy hand wrapped in gauze. I watched sullenly as Tommy and the others battled it out in the hula-hoop contest, with a Cracker Jack prize for the winner in each age group. Later, slurping on a cold piece of watermelon, I thought about how the holiday had been ruined for me, and I vowed revenge upon Allen. Let's see. Chinese water torture. Chinese finger torture. Chinese nutcracker torture. Chinese . . .

But as I calculated several devious devices of death for him, dusk settled suddenly over the landscape. It was time. Time for adults across the nation to pile kids into cars and drive to nearby parks and lakesides. Time for the annual anticipation felt by members of all the generations, from grandparents to toddlers. It was time for fireworks.

And so, spread-eagled on musty blankets, sticky mosquito repellent on our arms and legs, we stared skyward at the multi-colored display with its ferocious soundtrack, "oohing" and "aahing" at each new explosion. And as the last puff of white gunpowder drifted like an errant cloud across the black curtain of sky, and the final boom died in the distance, we silently thanked God that we were Americans.

On the way home, Tommy and Linda slept, snoring to the rhythm of the swiftly gliding car as it swallowed up the country miles. I, meanwhile, gazed out the open window and pondered the day's events. In spite of my injured hand—and pride—it had been a Fourth of July like no other, and the memory of its magic kept me awake well into the waning night. When the next day dawned, the morning sun peeking through the curtains to prod me awake, I turned over and went back to sleep. Was there any good reason to get up?

CHAPTER 5

"LAUGH YOUR TROUBLES AWAY!"

Two-ton Baker didn't actually weigh that much. But he was a very large man. It was more than a little impressive for kids to see him on TV, the eternal man-child taking up an entire two-seater on a roller coaster as he shouted at us: "Come ride! Laugh your troubles away!" He was a catalyst for Tommy and me, who endlessly harassed our father to take us to Riverview, the "World's Largest Amusement Park."

Opened in 1904, Riverview had established itself by the fifties as one of Chicago's North Side landmarks, its Pair-O-Chutes tower dominating the skyline. Kids who grew up in the city had only to take a bus or trolley to the colorful main entrance, and many who lived nearby simply walked. Living in the suburbs, we waited patiently until the evening when my dad arrived home from work and announced—always a surprise—"I'm taking you guys to Riverview tonight."

This time, Johnny was invited to join us. We three slid into the back seat, and Linda squeezed between our parents in the front. Upon arrival, our first thrill was driving beneath the Silver Flash roller coaster to reach the parking lot. "Speed up, Dad! No, no, slow down!" Timing was everything. The passage beneath the mountain of white wood had to coincide with the coaster's plummet. Go-Stop-Jerk-Stop-Jerk. The blaring of angry horns from behind was swiftly cut off by the fearful clatter of the vibrating structure and the joyous screams of the train's riders. Aah, a perfect entrance.

Once inside, we strolled easily through the hypnotized crowd. The park's myriad sights and sounds bombarded our senses on a sweltering summer's eve. A clamor of confusion punctuated by a crescendo of screams. The setting sun, a fireball on the horizon. Uniformed sailors with painted ladies on their arms. The photo gallery with its crescent moon smiling out at us. Black men falling into water-filled tanks. The "whoosh" of the Shoot-the-Chutes splashing into its pond. The ominous "click-click-click" of roller coaster chains everywhere. The sonorous, booming voice of the Midway barker seducing us toward the Palace of Wonders: "Step right up, ladies and gentlemen! You've never seen anything like this before! A woman with the body of an alligator! You won't believe it until you've seen it with your own eyes! And you'll be as close to her as I am to you right now!"

Thanks, but no thanks.

We had not come to see the freaky people such as Popeye—use your imagination—or to lose our money playing the rigged games of chance or to spend all night in the Skee-Ball building in order to earn enough tickets for a cheap toy; we had come to ride the rides. Any ride would do, but the coasters were our passion.

Moving up the Midway, we laid eyes on Riverview's newest coaster, the Fireball. Painted fire engine red, it boasted a hundred miles per hour for its take-off as it roared down its first hill into a pitch-dark tunnel. The TV commercials that touted this electrifying speed lied by about thirty miles per hour, but nobody cared.

Tommy and Johnny climbed into one low-slung car while I wisely sat next to my dad, knowing instinctively that he would somehow manage to save me when I was catapulted out into the night sky. Mom and Linda, never the fools, watched in trepidation from safe ground below. Following the slow ascent and a swift shot above the treetops, we found ourselves poised at the top of the first hill, the tunnel's mouth gaping at us in hungry anticipation. But not for long. Cursing under our breaths, we dove. Our thighs slammed upward to greet the safety bar, raising us in our seats. The tunnel's roof lurched out, decapitation in mind. Blasting into the cool darkness, we heard the maddening echoes of our own screams until, mercifully, we were ejected out into the hot air. And that was just the opening round.

The fact that we had now survived the Fireball gave us bragging rights in our neighborhood. However, it didn't relieve us of the ultimate duty of every male child born into a Chicago-area family. "One day, my son," my father once said to me, "you will ride the Bobs. Only then will you become a man."

This heartfelt wisdom aside, there were several obstacles placed before the virgin rider. The most serious of these was that every kid in the city and suburbs knew the unholy truth about the Bobs. It had taken a human life. This was no urban legend, either. It was a documented fact that a deranged passenger, showing off for friends as they watched his train climb the chain from the safety of the pavement below, had wiggled his way out of his safety bar, stood up, turned around, and waved "goodbye" to them. It turned out to be a final "good-bye." As the Bobs charged down its first hill, the man flew out of one side of the car and landed on another section of the coaster's track below. What no one knew for sure was whether he had died on impact or seconds later when another train ran him over. Either way, he became, in one mad moment, a statistic and a story, embellished around many a campfire as the years went by.

Another obstacle, even for those who had already mastered Riverview's other coasters, was the Bobs' notoriously twisting track, which left riders desperately clutching any article that wasn't attached, and a few that were. First-timers, Tommy and I—we had left Johnny behind with a sudden "headache"—stood petrified on the loading platform staring at a gigantic treasure chest filled with various items lost by riders over the years. A king's crown adorned with jewels sat atop the pile. Beneath it rested eyeglasses, hats, scarves, watches, necklaces, and—according to myth—a bra or two buried in its deepest recesses. If possessions were not lost, then painful cuts, scrapes, and bruises were gained. As my brother and I found out that fateful night.

Pushing last-second fears aside, we boarded rapidly so as not to change our muddled minds. From then on, everything was a blur. Shooting out of the station. Gliding past gorgeous flower gardens, symbolic funeral arrangements for the doomed riders. Clutching white-knuckled the sweaty safety bar. Ascending. Holding a reverential silence in honor of the one who had come before us who had not made it to the other side of the hill. The crest. Breathless pause. The chasm below us. Then . . .

Heavily padded seats could not protect us from being tossed around like rag dolls. Vicious curves and sudden twists slammed us soundly into each other. This violent meeting of flesh and bone was nothing new for this beast. Tommy and I were hurled back and forth with each buck of its rugged back and each flick of its mighty tail. Our fun had quickly evolved into survival at all costs.

Extending his elbow outward, Tommy landed a savage shot to my ribcage, causing me to gasp for breath. The little bastard. He did that on purpose. As the train banked into its next turn, I shifted my body, raised my own elbow, and let physics do the rest. Blood exploded into the air as Tommy screamed in genuine pain. Oh, shit, I thought. I've killed him. Dad will never take me to Riverview again.

The coaster came to a stop, and Tommy was helped out of his seat by the workers. Tears welled up in his eyes. Blood trickled down his arm. My blow had landed squarely on a week-old scab.

"I'm tellin'," he cried.

"No. No. Bad idea," I pleaded. "Dad'll never take us to Riverview again. Besides, you started it."

Our parents were summoned, and it was determined that Tommy would need emergency help. This freak "accident" allowed my family a once-in-a-lifetime opportunity to ride in the Riverview Park ambulance. This

would be so cool, I thought. Another high-speed thrill
ride. It wasn't. With sirens screaming and lights flashing, the vehicle "cruised" along at speeds of about three
miles per hour, a fugitive clown car from a nearby circus.
Patrons quickly cleared a path to allow us to pass, staring
in horror at the windows to catch a glimpse of the muti-
lated victims of some ride gone berserk. Tommy, Johnny,
and I did not disappoint. Always amused at our own antics, we "played dead" for the on-lookers, pressing our
faces against the glass, necks limp, eyes shut, tongues
lolling out of our mouths. My father looked over, saw
what we were up to, and said, "That's it. I'm never taking
you guys to Riverview again!"

After Tommy's arm had been patched up, we headed
back out to mingle with the crowd. Approaching the back
end of the Bowery, Johnny unexpectedly proclaimed, "I'd
like to try the Pair-O-Chutes! Who wants to go with me?"

"What?"

This was the kid who had chickened out on the Bobs,
and now he wanted to ride the most terrifying ride in the
history of the world? A ride famous for not operating
on windy days for fear of passengers ending up in Lake
Michigan? It defied all logic. It defied all common sense.
It defied the ancient writings of the prophets: "Thou shalt
not do stupid, life-threatening things."

In fact, entire generations of Chicagoans had avoided
the Pair-O-Chutes for one simple reason: the mere
thought of being seated on a small slab of wood with one
pathetic safety strap, dragged two hundred feet into the
air, and released into a "free fall" that was brutally halted
by a gigantic spring mechanism that jerked riders to a
violent stop scared the crap out of sensible people. Obviously, I didn't have the brains I was born with.

"All right," I said. "I'll go with you. But what about
Tommy?" I turned to look at him.

With hurt eyes, he returned my gaze. "I can't. My
arm . . ." He held up the bandaged appendage.

"Big baby."

"Mom . . ."

"Shh," I shushed him. "Look, don't say anything, and I'll take you in Aladdin's Castle as soon as we get off." Provided they don't have to peel our bodies off the concrete, I thought.

"Okay," he said, half smiling. Tommy loved the castle.

Johnny and I nervously waited in a forty-minute line and climbed onto the seat, our legs dangling. Ascending, we were treated to a spectacular view of the city at night. Johnny, who apparently had a death wish, kept turning around to see more of the lights, causing us to sway. Eventually, we sat silent-still, perched precariously, lifted higher and higher and higher . . . The white canvas exploded noisily above our heads, and the floor dropped out of the universe.

I learned something about gravity that night. The seat fell first, my bottom next. I figured the seat had simply broken off, and we were dropping to our deaths. When we made solid contact again—about halfway down—it was like being whacked with a paddle, so forceful was the initial blow. Screaming madly, we continued our insane plunge. Without warning, the spring mechanism clutched us, stretching us out like tired rubber bands and snapping us up again until we were shaken to a stop. Stepping off, we staggered unsteadily toward the rest of our group.

"Let's go home," I suggested, completely rattled.

"What?" said my father, laughing. "Don't tell me that kiddie ride was too much for you young men?"

"Uh-huh," mumbled a woozy Johnny.

"What about the castle?" Tommy hissed in my ear.

Looking up, I saw the resolve in his face. Clearly, he was not taking "no" for an answer.

"Okay. Just let me catch my breath." It had been a stomach-churning night thus far, and I well knew the castle would not settle me down.

Actually, there were two fun houses at Riverview: the aforementioned Aladdin and its antithesis, the House of Hades. In fact, the single most famous Chicago urban legend came courtesy of Hades. Supposedly, a man had stumbled from its exit one day with poisonous snakes attached to every part of his body. He had collapsed, twitching in agony, and died right there on the sunlit Midway. It's no wonder we avoided Hades like the Ten Plagues of Egypt, opting instead for the thrill of Aladdin's eccentric abode, his larger-than-life visage with movable eyes greeting every guest who dared to enter.

And what a fun house it was: a maze of screen doors, tilted rooms, a gallery of mirrors, a barrel roll, and the "magic carpet" finale. Its nastiest "surprise," however, was reserved for ladies only. At one point along the wondrous journey, everyone had to walk single file up a flight of stairs positioned outside in close proximity to Aladdin's beard. A man sat discreetly above the ticket booth facing the castle. When an unsuspecting woman in a skirt—common apparel for social outings back then—reached the top of the steps, the trigger-happy employee would simply push a button. This released jet streams from hidden "air holes," causing the woman's skirt to billow up above her waist, flapping into her face. A rank of sailors, standing by the black iron fence surrounding the castle, would hoot and howl in horny delight as the red-faced woman fought to regain her shredded dignity. My mom hated Aladdin.

That evening, in a blood pact sealed earlier that summer, Tommy, Johnny, and I entered the castle with the explicit purpose of conquering the barrel roll, the most difficult of all feats. The old woman who jealously guarded the barrel did not allow just anyone to go through it. As pre-teens, we were considered too young and frail. This time we would not suffer the humiliation of her croaking at us, "You're too little! Walk around!" This time we'd fight for our rights.

"But we've ridden the Bobs!"

"Don't matter," she retorted smugly, her three remaining teeth protruding crookedly from her wet gums. "You're too little; you'll get hurt! Now, walk around!"

Arms crossed in defiance, we refused to budge. "We paid our money!"

"A dime each!"

Seeing we were not about to acquiesce, she reluctantly nodded her head. "All right, get in. But you'll be sorry."

We entered the barrel for the first time in our lives. Seeing its shiny smoothness looming ahead like the muzzle of a cannon, quiet and still, gave us a false sense of confidence. The ancient woman slowly pulled the giant lever behind her, and the barrel began to rotate. We moved quickly forward, bracing ourselves with our hands and feet, remembering the warning of our older friends: "Keep moving. Don't stop for a second or you're going down!"

Halfway through. "This is easy!" I boasted loudly to the others behind me. My last intelligible words. Looking ahead, I saw, framed in the barrel's mouth, the demented face of the old woman. She reached her withered hand back for the speed lever. Ramming it to the floor, she cackled in triumph.

The next sound I heard was the crack of my head against solid wood. Then came the staccato sounds of cracking elbows, knees, and heads as the three of us hit the deck in a spin cycle, a Moe-Larry-Curly nightmare of panic and pain. The barrel stopped suddenly. We crawled out, wounded warriors nauseous from the ceaseless spinning, desperate for fresh air.

The crone flashed us a merciless grin. "Next time I tell you to walk around, you'll walk around, won't you?" Thus ended the lesson.

Later, as we headed through the parking lot to the car, I shook off the dizziness and reflected on the night's glories. I had taken courage to a new level and would forever mark this odyssey for its series of firsts. Watching the lights fade into the distance as the car moved further away, I naively assumed that Riverview would always stand proud. Less than a decade later, however, ball and crane made mournful music together as Aladdin's eyes, forever stilled, sadly watched the destruction of this magical place. And as the years passed, whenever hot summer nights assailed us, we imagined a large, friendly man calling out: "Come ride! Laugh your troubles away!"

CHAPTER 6

"NIGHTTIME IS THE RIGHT TIME"

"Come in when the street lights come on," was an oft-repeated phrase of the era. Intoned by mothers and fathers across suburbia, its purpose was two-fold. First, it was used as a basic time device. Save for the occasional Mickey Mouse watch, used mostly as a showpiece, kids didn't wear watches. And they certainly didn't keep track of time. But the street lights were infallible; they always blinked on as darkness approached. Thus, kids across America always knew when to head home.

The second purpose for that simple statement was more ominous. Our parents were warning us: "Come in or else . . ." Because only a fool could miss the lights as they stuttered to life, it was assumed that, if a child didn't come in, he was being disobedient. Therefore, yelling-screaming-grounding-whipping-beating was in order. Another, more subtle, "or else . . ." had to do with what terrible fate awaited us if we stayed out after dark. We could be abducted by aliens, mangled by monsters, or devoured by demon dogs. God knows our imaginations were such that any sound or shadow would spook us into scurrying for the comforting lights of home. So, all in all, it was a tried and true system, one that benefited both parent and child alike.

Occasionally, however, there was a lapse in judgment, and we stayed out late. This usually involved some game that was more fun in the dark. One of the best was "Fifty Scatter." This required one kid to lean against a parkway tree, his eyes pressed into his forearm, and count aloud from one to fifty. Meanwhile, the other kids would "scatter." Thus, the clever name. The person who was "it" then yelled, "Here I come, ready or not!" But this was no ordinary hide-and-seek. The object was for the "hiders" to jump out whenever the spirit moved them and run to the tree. If they touched it before they were tagged, they were "safe"; if not, they were "it" for the next game.

There were several strategies for those in hiding. One, usually employed by speedsters like Jimmy and Greg, was to wait behind a tree or a garage wall and then suddenly spring out at the surprised searcher, zooming past him before he could react. Others hid in clever places, such as behind the wheel of a parked car in the street or in the center of a big clump of bushes, jumping out only after the hunter had wandered off in the opposite direction. Slow runners, like Eddie and me, crawled beneath a wheelbarrow or behind a hedge and lay flat until somebody else had been caught.

Our favorite nighttime game, however, was "Ding Dong Ditch." This entailed dumping leaves and twigs inside some unsuspecting neighbor's screen door and then ringing the doorbell and running. The riskiest version of this activity involved hiding in clandestine places within view of the front door in order to witness the reaction of the irate homeowner. This increased the thrill because of the very real possibility of being spotted. Since the entire block knew each other, this would lead to identification and a quick phone call home, resulting in our untimely deaths.

"Hello, Hank. This is Roger Anderson down the block. Some kids dumped leaves inside my door and rang the bell. I looked around and saw your children crouching behind Bill Watt's old Ford across the street. When I went after them, they took off. I didn't want to call the police, so . . ."

"Look, I'm really sorry, Roger. Don't worry. I'll take care of it. They won't bother you again."

Thus, the goal of the game: don't get caught. One mid-August night, however, we almost did just that. Having obtained permission to stay out late, Tommy and I teamed with Johnny to take "Ding Dong Ditch" to its ultimate level.

We started with old Mrs. Dartman's house across the street from Johnny's. An easy target, she stormed out onto her lawn and looked up and down the block while we lay flat behind a giant parkway bush and giggled. "Who's out there?" she demanded in a slightly terrified voice. "What do you want?"

Obviously, we wanted to watch her stand in her front yard in a purple housecoat and reading glasses screaming into the dark until, shaking violently, she scampered back into the safety of her house, slamming the wooden door behind her.

"Ha. Ha," laughed Johnny. "That was fun. 'What do you want? What do you want?'" he mocked. "We should have yelled out, 'We want to murder you!' She would have had a heart attack."

We brayed like the jackasses we were.

"Hey, I've got an idea." There was a gleam in Johnny's eyes. "Why don't we hit Mr. Connor's place?"

Tommy and I stared in amazement at our misguided friend. "Are you crazy?" I asked. "Do you want to die young?"

Every neighborhood had a Mr. Connor. He and his wife had no children. This was a good thing. Mr. Connor hated children. He sat at his living room window all day while Mrs. Connor knitted, watching for a stray child to set foot on his no-blade-of-grass-out-of-place lawn. Then, in a burst of fury, he charged like a horse in heat to chase the hapless child away. It was rumored that he owned a revolver and wouldn't hesitate to use it on a nighttime prowler. Legend had it that Corey McMahon, a teenage greaser who lived two blocks over, walked with a limp from just such an encounter.

"I think it'd be great," argued Johnny. "He'd never think we had the nerve to do it."

True, I thought. Gun-wielding sociopaths seldom worried about cocky kids having the balls to vandalize their homes.

"I'm not goin'," stated Tommy, crossing his arms over his chest.

"Chicken," crooned Johnny.

"You're insane," I said. "Let's just go back to Mrs. Dartman's."

Johnny finally wore us down. We couldn't keep after the same poor old lady. She'd go nuts and call the cops. And everybody else on the block knew us too well. Even if Mr. Connor looked out and saw us running away, he wouldn't have a clue as to our identity. To him, all children looked the same. And besides, it would give us bragging rights for years. Not even crazy Jimmy could pull off a feat like this.

Johnny was right. We'd attain Superman status for this stunt. "Okay, we'll go," I said half-heartedly, "but you're putting the leaves in."

"Don't worry. I can handle it."

And so we gathered a handful of leaves, some sticks, and, for good measure, a bit of dirt, piling it into Johnny's cupped hands. Then, we began our slow, stealthy stroll up the quiet street. God, what were we doing?

Mr. Connor's house sat across the street about five or six houses away from our "base camp." The plan was to do the deed, bolt back to our side, and sprint to the fortress of Johnny's back yard. It should have worked flawlessly.

Breathing heavily, we stood statue-like. We were lucky. The front door was closed and the drapes were drawn, a lamp shining dimly from within. Without a word, we tread onto the lawn, where Tommy and I froze. Using sign language, we signaled to Johnny to continue. Much to his credit, the brave little bugger moved to the front steps, climbed them, looked back at us, winked, and carefully opened the screen door. To this day, I'm not sure what distracted me. Most likely some common noise. I wheeled around, searching for the source. Dog? cat? neighbor? killer?

The next thing I knew, Tommy was no longer beside me. He and Johnny were halfway across the street in a dead run. I looked up at the house. Nothing had changed. The front door was still closed; the drapes were still drawn. No one was stirring. Cowards, I thought. "Captain Courageous" must have turned yellow at the last minute. I stared at the fleeing figures. Johnny glanced back over his shoulder and seemed to read in my eyes the scornful amusement. His answer to my glare shook me to my soul.

"I rang the bell!"

I spun around in mindless fear to see the shadowy silhouette of Mr. Connor framed in the porch light. He leapt toward me with outstretched arms. "I'll kill ya!"

I turned and ran for my life, sprinting past my partners like Jesse Owens in his prime. "Here he comes!"

Now, it was every man for himself. We scattered in different directions. I took off up Johnny's driveway toward the maze of back yards that we knew so well, a million hiding places beckoning me. Convinced Mr. Connor's footsteps were close behind me, I streaked through Johnny's yard, across the next lot, and slid down a small incline to nestle in the thick undergrowth of some overgrown bushes. Peering fearfully out into the night, I saw nothing. From that point on, I assumed a corpse-like stillness. The only sound emanating from my makeshift grave was that of short bursts of breath as my heart hammered against my chest. Sweat rolled down my forehead, stinging my eyes. Hungry mosquitoes feasted on my face and neck, but I didn't dare defend myself. I was a prisoner of my own folly. But where were the others? Had they been taken?

Suddenly, a crash, a crack, and a high-pitched scream. Dear God, the massacre was beginning. I stared out from my secret shelter. Johnny, in the dark, had missed an opening in a row of sturdy bushes and been catapulted into the air, landing solidly on the hard ground. He had pulled himself up and was now running awkwardly, his eyes bulging out and blood streaming down his injured leg. I desperately wanted to call out to him, to welcome him into my safe haven, but this was war. Above all, I had to save myself.

About four hours later—more likely ten minutes—I crawled out of my insect-infested hole, grass-stains and mud covering my jeans, and began searching for my companions. It didn't take long. Johnny was sitting, his back resting against the cherry tree behind the garage, tending to his wounded shin with a wad of Kleenex. Tommy, hands on knees, stood above him, looking worried.

"Where is he?" I whispered, startling them.

"I never saw him," said Tommy, who told us he had split off from us and eventually climbed a tree to hide.

"I think he was chasing me," said Johnny. "I was running so fast, I never saw the damn bush. I slammed right into it."

"I heard you," I sympathized.

"What're we gonna do?" moaned Tommy, scared down to his socks.

"I'm goin' in," said Johnny. The blood had slowed to a trickle.

"What about us?" I protested, all the while thinking about how this had been his dumb-ass idea in the first place. "We have to cross the street to get home."

"Go through the back yards and cross at the intersection. If he spots you, he'll think you're somebody comin' home from another direction. Besides, he's probably home by now."

As usual, Johnny's logic seemed unassailable.

So, we said our good-byes and watched our friend hobble through the screen door. His parents would never know. He would concoct a story about some normal "boys-will-be-boys" accident, and they would treat him with Bactine and a Band-Aid, give him a heaping bowl of ice cream, and tuck him into bed. Meanwhile, Tommy and I had to creep home like escaping convicts across a prison yard, all the while trying to avoid psycho-man from down the street.

We almost made it. We were approaching the intersection and could see our house in the near distance. We stepped cautiously into the street light's glare.

"Hey, you kids! Stop right there! What are your names? Where do you live?"

Mr. Connor had been standing by the pole. We had never seen him. Too tired to run, we faced him. He looked worn-out and grumpy, as if we had rudely pulled him away from an episode of "The Untouchables." Unlike Eliot Ness, he carried no weapon, and I sensed he wanted to be home as much as we did.

"C'mon. Tell me your names."

Glancing swiftly at Tommy, I stammered, "I'm Jimmy O'Donnell."

Tommy fielded the ruse. "And I'm Eddie Davis. We both live down there." He pointed down the street toward our friends' houses.

Next, ever agreeable, we supplied him with their phone numbers as well.

After warning us that our parents would be hearing from him tomorrow, he allowed us to leave, watching us saunter in shame, heads hung, to our new homes. Aiding our cause, Jimmy and Eddie had the misfortune of camping out at Greg's that night, making them vulnerable to a frame-up. Apparently, without an alibi, they both received whippings at the hands of their fathers, never a pretty sight.

There is no moral to this story. We lied that night because that's what kids do. We did, however, refrain from calling on any more neighbors that summer, not because we felt bad about what had happened to Jimmy and Eddie, but for fear it might happen to us.

We spent the entire Labor Day block party avoiding Mr. Connor. And when the sun finally sank, another summer

sank with it. It seemed like only yesterday that the days
had stretched out in front of us like so many Sioux warriors on Custer's horizon. But, incredibly, these halcyon
days had been swept off our landscape, and only school,
bleak and foreboding, stared back into our sullen faces.
Tomorrow we would trade our bats and gloves for No. 2
pencils and sheets of loose-leaf paper and, as the days got
shorter, wonder if the summer sun had ever burned above
us in the cloudless afternoon sky.

PART II
FALL

CHAPTER 7

"A MANY-SPLENDORED THING"

I strode anxiously into Mr. Paducci's fifth grade class-room on the second floor of the red brick building and sat down. This was the last year I would ever be at Frank-lin D. Roosevelt Elementary. Next fall, I would have to ride on the bus with chain-smoking hooligans to the junior high on the other side of town. But now, sitting and glancing around at the other students, I took comfort in familiar faces. There was Tony, whose Catholic parents used the rhythm method for birth control, albeit not very successfully; they had produced seventeen chil-dren in almost as many years. While other boys wore neatly pressed collared shirts and slacks, Tony dressed in tattered hand-me-downs. In the front row was Albert, the child prodigy pianist with a bucktoothed smile and horn-rimmed glasses, who regaled each year's class with ever more proficient playing. Destined for greatness, his heroes were Bach and Beethoven. Over by the window, slumped silently at his desk, was Sammy. His life had been forever changed one sad day in second grade when, riding his bike home for lunch, he had almost been killed by a hit-and-run driver. Once smooth and gregarious, he now stuttered when he spoke.

Oh, no, not Dale. My eyes locked on a tall boy sitting in the last row by the door. Held back after first grade, Dale was the class bully. He ran a huge hand through slick, black hair and scowled at me as if to say, "Come recess, I'm putting a cigarette out in your face."

Spotting Ralph and Doug sitting near each other brought one particular second grade memory rush-ing back. Doug had been a leader even then. Prim and proper, he had daily recited the Pledge of Allegiance as if Eisenhower himself was looking on. He had an affable personality and was generally looked up to by his peers. But on this one occasion, he went too far.

Mrs. Breckin's second graders were learning about the value of a dollar. To illustrate, she had us work for weeks on a class project. First, we constructed a cardboard "grocery store" complete with shelves. Second, we were told to bring in packages, boxes, and cans of various food items, which were neatly arranged to be sold. Finally, we were assigned parts in one big Americana production. Some of us would be shoppers—Ralph and I were in this group—using Monopoly money and wooden pieces of change marked "50," "25," "10," "5," and "1" to make our purchases. Another group of peasants would get to bag the groceries. An elite few, including Doug the Patriot, would get the privilege of being grocers: taking orders, adding up totals, and making change.

Doug, playing his part to perfection, would take someone's order by snatching a pencil from behind his ear and asking cheerfully, "And how may I help you today?" Then, he would write with precision on a notepad the customer's order and bark it out to his overworked underlings. "Miss Johnson would like two cans of corn, three cans of chicken noodle soup, two boxes of Rice Krispies, and a package of Oreos! And step on it!"

"Eat my boogers, Doug," whispered Ralph, a sentiment shared by those of us outside the corridors of power.

Doug continued to harass laborers and customers alike—"I'm sorry, Miss Jenkins, but we don't carry that brand of toilet paper"—until Mrs. Breckin mercifully called a halt to our learning.

"All right, boys and girls, that's enough for today. Go put on your wraps."

As Ralph and I headed for the coat racks, we glanced back at Doug. There he was, in all his pompous pride, taking inventory. Enough was enough. Without any thought—clearly—we walked purposefully over to the store and toppled it, boxes and all, on top of Doug. Cans clattered across the dirty tile as the red and white build-ing crashed to the floor. Buried beneath the debris was the now wailing dictator, having been brought to his knees by the people's revolution.

Mrs. Breckin did not see it that way. Amidst the laugh-ter, she swept down vulture-like and clasped Doug's collar, heaving him out of the pile. Then, she cornered Ralph and me. Not amused, she chose to keep both of us after school to write punishment. So we wrote. And wrote. And wrote.

Asked to write how we felt about hurting Doug's feel-ings—as well as almost maiming him—Ralph wrote "I feel like a rocket ship" thirty-six times, threw a temper tantrum, tore up his paper, and refused to finish. I thought it just as well because Mrs. Breckin probably wouldn't have been too keen on the "rocket ship" thing. I wrote "I am sorry" fifty times, turned it in, was told it was not neat enough, and sat back down to write it out another fifty times. All the while, Tommy, waiting outside for me to walk him home from kindergarten, stood forlornly in the rain and waved at me through the window.

I flashed back to my senses as Mary Linder walked gracefully into the fifth grade classroom. Her blond hair, curled at the bottom, bounced lightly with every step she took. She smiled at me, and I almost melted in my seat. Ever since first grade, when I had chased her with scis-sors for messing with my toothpick art, I had been en-amored of her. And the thought of being able to stare at her for an entire school year instead of only at recess was almost too much to take in. No doubt about it. Heaven shined its light on me that day.

My brief history at Roosevelt Elementary had not been that of a model student. In fact, during one dismal stretch in fourth grade, disciplinary notes to my mom had begun piling up under the evergreens next to a house on the shortcut home. But this was a new start with a new teacher. A male teacher.

I had been rather disdainful of my female teachers over the years. They were always quick to strike, especially if their target was a boy. Mr. Paducci, on the other hand, had a reputation for being cool. We had witnessed him at recess actually playing softball or tossing a football around with the boys in his class. And who could forget last fall when the White Sox had hosted the Dodgers in the first game of the World Series? While Mrs. Quantrell gagged us on vocabulary, the cheers from just down the hall, where Mr. Paducci allowed his class to watch the game, resonated in our ears. And, best of all, we had heard that, if he caught you talking or daydreaming in class, he would not humiliate you by sending you to the principal's office; he would merely fling a chalk-loaded eraser at you.

Fifth grade would also be the last year with the desks that opened to reveal a space for all our supplies: pencils, pens, erasers, crayons, rulers, paper, scissors, glue, and textbooks for language, history, math, science, and health. Mr. Paducci also initiated our own classroom library and encouraged us to bring in books from home so others could check them out. This system allowed me to wallow weekly in a new Hardy Boys adventure, a springboard to my life-long love of books. Dale the Bully scoffed at reading, preferring to spend his time learning real-life skills such as lighting matches and carving obscenities into his desk with a knife. But one time he snuck a *Playboy* magazine into our library, causing quite a stir. Spewing righteous anger, Mr. Paducci locked the offensive material in the closet. We never saw it again.

Instead, we struggled through science, mostly learning about the world of nature. Mr. Paducci told us we would all get to dissect a pig embryo in junior high, giving us yet another good reason for wanting to stay in fifth grade forever. We also studied parts of speech, Lewis and Clark, food pyramids, and something called new math.

Sociology, not included in the curriculum, was learned "hands on" every day on the playground. This is where it all came to the surface, every bit of deviant, sociopathic, psychotic, push-me-again-and-I'll-rip-your-face-off behavior. Kids were picked on for being too short, too tall, too fat, too thin, shy, smart, dumb, awkward, tomboys, Nancy-boys, and Boy Scouts. The innocent-looking asphalt square with its bike racks, jungle gym, and swing set, bordered by fields of brown grass and dirt diamonds, was much like a prison yard: no one could escape, and it was survival of the fittest, so watch your back. Harmless childhood games such as freeze tag, blind man's bluff, and red rover took on sinister dimensions. At any time, a kid could lose it, and a fight would break out. These playground pugilists would batter each other senseless in front of a bloodthirsty crowd of shouting spectators until a weary teacher stepped in to stop it.

Also common were freakish casualties. Kids jumped off swings and sprained ankles, fell off slides and broke collarbones, tripped playing tag and knocked out front teeth. Once Ziggy Zimmerman caught a flying baseball bat to the forehead that required thirty stitches. And when Bobo Taylor got his fat head stuck in a bike rack, the firemen had to come to his rescue. It was a mine field out there.

Kids threw up too. Seemingly every day. Frank Mazeroski—no relation to the Pittsburgh second baseman—ran the bases too soon after lunch and hurled the remains of his tuna salad sandwich into the rusted metal trash can behind the backstop. Wiry little Al Sanderson got sick on top of the monkey bars and rained wet globs of peanut butter and marshmallow fluff onto unsuspecting victims below.

Above all, the psychological terror of the playground was at its apex when kids got their grubby little hands on colored chalk. Normally used for hopscotch, it could easily be turned into a weapon of revenge, the Internet of its time. Virtually anything about anybody could be scrawled on a slab of concrete, a mass media message to the world:

Rob loves Carolyn
Wally's mother wears combat boots
Chris picks his nose and eats it

And these tabloid headlines would remain until the next downpour washed them into oblivion, leaving only the emotional scars behind.

One bright fall afternoon, I rushed out for recess. Around me, kids broke into small groups to play four square, jump rope, teeter-totter, swing, or slide.

I headed out to the field, where a gang was gathering for a game of touch football. Suddenly, a gaggle of girls caught my eye. Giggling, they were pointing at some chalk markings on the sidewalk that led to the school's front entrance. When one of them pointed at me, they all laughed loudly. Oh, dear God. What could this mean?

After they ran off to play, I snuck over to see the prophecy for myself. There it was, printed in block letters: MIKE B. LOVES MARY L. The scoundrel had used blue for the names and pink for the "LOVES." I was doomed. The *Tribune* and the *Sun-Times* would have the full story tomorrow. The local TV stations would have expanded coverage on the nightly news. I would have to convince my family to move to Oregon.

"What have we here?"

It was the voice of Doug. He and Ralph had seen me transfixed and had sauntered up behind me.

I spun around. "Don't say anything," I pleaded to the boy with the biggest mouth in the fifth grade. "You guys gotta help me. How do I get it to come off?"

"Some cleaning product, I suppose," snickered Doug.

"You could always pee on it," laughed Ralph. "That would wash it off."

"Oh, you're no help," I whined. "Don't you get it? If Mary sees this, my life is over. I can never go back to class."

"Well," said Doug, "I guess you could use a squirt gun. If you had one."

I looked up to see Doug smirking and patting his coat pocket with his hand.

I lunged at him. "Give it to me!"

"Not so fast. It'll cost you. A dime. To borrow it."

"But that's my ice cream money."

"Like it or lump it."

"Okay, okay." I pulled the small coin from my pants pocket and reluctantly handed it to the mercenary boy.

Doug, in turn, handed over my salvation. "Oh, by the way," he said, casually flipping and catching my dime as he and Ralph walked away, "you'll have to load it yourself."

Shit. An empty, useless firearm. Now, I had a mission impossible ahead of me: I must sneak into the building, fill the squirt gun with water from the drinking fountain, and hurry back outside without being spotted. Let's see. How many school rules was I violating? No going into the building during recess; no trips to the water cooler without permission; no squirt guns allowed on the premises. Great. This should keep me in fifth grade for another year or two.

I moved swiftly. Mr. Paducci was all-time quarterback for the scrimmage, so I was sure he wouldn't see me. Covering my face with my jacket, I made my way in a surreptitious manner toward the door. The Headless Horseman on the prowl. Glancing around one last time, I pulled on the handle and let myself into the sleepy building. I paused and listened. Nothing. Quietly crept up the stairs. Listened again. Nothing. Not a sound. I could see the shiny silver drinking fountain gleaming like an oasis at the far end of the hall. I walked on tiptoe, each step exploding like the crash of cymbals in the stifling stillness. Sweat ran in rivers off the sides of my face. Unmolested, I reached my goal, quickly filled the gun with water, and shoved it securely into my pants pocket. Might as well get a drink while I'm here. No one had ever earned one more.

"What are you doing in here?"

This time, the sonorous voice behind me belonged to our principal, Mr. Harmon.

"I had to use the restroom," I blurted out, choking on a swallow of water. "It was an emergency."

Mr. Harmon stared sternly down at me. His eyes came to rest on my pants. "Apparently so."

Instinctively, I grabbed hold of my pants leg. It was soaking wet. The squirt gun was leaking. Help me, Jesus.

"Why don't you get into the boys' room and clean yourself up?"

"Yes, Mr. Harmon. Yes, sir. That's what I'll do, sir."

I shuffled away, duck-like, to the solace of the restroom. There, I patted my pants down with a handkerchief, refilled the defective squirt gun, thrust it into my jacket pocket this time, and ran outside, caring little who saw me.

Panting, I reached the graffiti-stained sidewalk and pumped away. The Lone Ranger himself never got off so many quick, deadly accurate shots. With a demonic smile, I watched the chalk lines blur until only a fuzzy outline remained. I jumped up and down several times, smearing the spot with the soles of my shoes. Out of breath, I stared down at the modern-art mess. Whatever it was now, it was illegible. Victory was mine.

As I sat stone-faced at my desk, hands covering my wet spot, my classmates filed past me to take their seats. The next thing I was aware of was a soft hand delicately touching my shoulder. I looked up into the gentle green eyes of Mary Linder. She leaned closer and whispered in my ear, "I saw it. I don't mind."

For the rest of the day, I sat stupefied, staring at the back of Mary's head two rows in front of me. If Mr. Paducci saw me, he never let fly with an eraser, choosing instead to allow a fifth grade Romeo to dream contentedly of his Juliet.

CHAPTER 8

"MOVIE MAYHEM"

Hazy smoke clouded the suburban landscape. The scent of burning leaves wafted through the chill autumn air. These were the signs of Saturday. By universal agreement, families banded together to rake leaves into neat piles and carry them via worn blankets and bed sheets to the makeshift pyres that dotted the bottoms of every driveway on our block. Fathers were in charge of the matches and supervising the blaze, which was constantly fueled by new bundles of crackling leaves. Mothers were the foremen, slicing the yard into sections and assigning kids to various areas, ruthlessly overseeing everything.

Tommy and I spent the morning raking, scooping, delivering, and dumping. By noon, the grass was visible again. Time to throw the football around, to run bizarre patterns for our dad to toss it past parkway trees and alongside parked cars. Imaginations overheated in the huddle by the blazing fire. "Okay, Dad, listen. Tommy will run to the elm tree and cut to the street. Fake it to him. I'll run through the gate, across the patio, around the willow tree, behind the garage, over the fence, through Mr. Smith's yard to the front lawn. Throw it over the roof, and I'll catch it."

Or, more likely, it would come screaming out of the sky like a Soviet missile, smash into my forehead, and put me in a coma for three months.

My father looked at me as if I was a gypsy child who had wandered onto his property. "What are you, nuts? Go out to the fire hydrant, and I'll lob it to you. See if you can hang on this time."

Eventually, as the fire burned down to gray ashes, we would tire and break for lunch. The Oscar Mayer Bologna sandwiches and Jays Potato Chips were set out on the picnic table. Seated on benches beneath the red maple, we chatted like ladies over coffee, washing down our meal with Kool-Aid.

"So, now that you've finished your chores, what're you up to this afternoon?" asked Dad. The answer lay in a thousand possibilities.

Suddenly, Johnny burst into the yard. "Hey, everybody!" The possibilities multiplied. "You guys wanna see a show?"

"Yeah," we answered in unison. Why hadn't we thought of that?

The Regal Theatre, our town's one and only movie house, stood in the heart of the downtown, a half block from the train station. It had stood there forever. Its brick facade concealed a modern lobby renovated a few years earlier. Its old-fashioned marquee, surrounded by light bulbs at night, shouted out the title of that week's film—only blockbusters like *Ben-Hur*, *The Ten Commandments*, and *Bridge On the River Kwai* were booked for two weeks. Admission was ninety cents for adults, thirty-five cents for kids twelve and under. Plain popcorn cost fifteen cents and came in a narrow, white box; the buttered variety cost a quarter and was packaged in a larger, yellow container. Generic root beer, cola, orange, and grape pop sold for a dime per cup—and don't forget to hold in the button if you wanted crushed ice.

If nighttime was well suited for a family outing, then Saturday matinees were a haven for kids. The theatre owners stoked this madness by occasionally booking double-feature action films—usually Westerns—or a "carnival of cartoons," one eight-minute animated short after another. Parents would drop their kids off for an afternoon of excitement or laughter, knowing they were being supervised in a safe, climate-controlled environment.

The supervisors, feared by all, were the ushers. They represented raw power in its purest form: teenagers in uniforms, flashlights for weapons. The third degree in the face or a not-so-subtle whack on the knee was all that was needed to subdue a noisy child. These sadists even hauled recalcitrant kids up the aisle through the swinging doors to the lobby, from whence the begging-for-mercy little ones never returned. It was rumored that there was a secret room behind the big, black door marked "Manager's Office" where kids were taken for beatings. No one we knew had ever seen the inside of this chamber of horrors, but its existence was never doubted.

It was here, within the walls of this majestic old theatre, that I had been baptized in comedy and horror, drama and suspense. It was where the Little Rascals cavorted; where Lady and the Tramp romanced each other; where the Lone Ranger and Tonto hunted down rustlers; and where Abbott and Costello met Frankenstein. Mickey, Donald, and Goofy made us laugh; nature films held us in awe; Movietone newsreels informed us about our world.

And if some of the supernatural fare wasn't scary enough in plot and character, then it was enlivened by the technology of 3D. We often sat mesmerized, right elbows cocked in the air, holding multi-colored cardboard "glasses" to our eyes as the ghosts became visible or a knife jetted out from the screen toward us. Johnny peed his pants once courtesy of a skeleton that shot fire from his fingertips.

So, on this particular Saturday, my dad agreed to drop off and pick up, allowing us to spend two and a half hours in "kid heaven."

"What's playing?" asked Tommy, not that it mattered.

"*Northwest Passage.*"

This was good. It was not a Western but the next best thing, an old movie about the French and Indian War starring Spencer Tracy. As long as there were guns, knives, and savages, we would not be bored.

"What's it about?" asked Mom, and we knew we were in trouble. "Is there violence in it?"

"I don't think so." Johnny was fast. "It's mostly about history, I think."

That our country's history was built on one bloody conflict after another always seemed to escape my mom. "Oh, history. Well, that should be educational then."

Grabbing our allowance money, we ran to the car before she could put two and two together, and we were off to yet another blood-soaked history lesson.

"Behave yourselves." This warning, spoken by my father as he dropped us off in front of the theatre, was not to be taken lightly. We knew that, wherever we went, we were expected to behave, or there would be hell to pay. It was this way always. If a teacher, neighbor, business owner, or any other adult reported our misbehavior to our parents . . .

"Okay, bye."

Stopping to buy our tickets, we hustled through the glass doors. The cold air smacked our faces. Mr. Harold, the venerable ticket taker—the only one we had ever known—tore our pink tickets in half and handed us the stubs.

"I wanna get a treat," said Johnny.

Springing forward, we eyed the smooth glass case that held every candy known to mankind: Dots, Black Crows, Good & Plenty, Good & Fruity, Tootsie Rolls, Snow Caps, and other movie sweets. Johnny's sister Patty had once eaten Bonomo's Turkish Taffy and pulled out two new silver fillings. Not a wise purchase.

"What're we gonna get?" asked Tommy, his nose pressed hard on the glass.

Ten minutes later, treats in hand, we headed down the aisle. We always sat in the same location: left side, aisle seats, five rows back. Occasionally, we broke from habit and moved up to front row center. The next day, our necks would be stiff, and our vision would be blurred. But it was worth it for bragging rights. "Oh, yeah, we sat in the front row for *Creature from the Black Lagoon*. Naw, we weren't a bit scared."

The theatre was packed, which was nothing new. It usually was on a Saturday afternoon. We dropped into our cushioned seats and, buoyed by the buzz of sugar-hyped children, stared in anticipation at the red velvet curtain. Tommy shoved Dots up his nose to amuse us while we waited.

Without fanfare, the curtain slid open. The crowd, amazingly, went silent. During the next half hour, we watched coming attractions, a Bugs Bunny cartoon, a travelogue, and a Movietone newsreel—Johnny left to get a pop; he was terrified of Khrushchev.

Once the feature began, we were spellbound. The film had everything: suspense, action, senseless violence. The neatest part was when a war-crazed soldier carried a severed Indian head in a bloody sack wherever he went. His fellow fighters would ask him, "Hey, what's in the sack?" He would just grin and lick his lips. And people wondered why our generation grew up to oppose the Vietnam War?

If it had been a perfect world, I would have stayed for the climax that day. The credits would have come up to a burst of applause, the houselights would have brightened, and we all would have tramped contentedly up the aisle, Black Crows stuck to the bottoms of our tennis shoes. But, alas, it was not to be. The Gestapo saw to that.

We had become intrigued with the young girl sitting next to her little brother in the row in front of ours. She constantly covered his eyes in an attempt to shield him from the relentless massacre on the screen.

I leaned forward. "What are you doing?"

"I don't want him to see this."

I glanced up at the screen—a close shot of an Indian warrior burying his tomahawk into the back of one of Rogers' Rangers. "Why not?"

Incredulous, she turned to face us. "Because . . . if you see blood, you'll turn bad."

That was too much. I laughed out loud, elbowing Tommy and Johnny. "Ha. Ha. Did you hear that?"

The bright spotlight beamed directly into my now frozen-in-fear face. The voice came out of the dark behind it. "Let's go, kid."

God help me. I had been caught in the act, talking during the movie. Surely, this was a minor transgression, not as fatal as being caught bouncing Juicy Fruit candies off someone's head or flinging a flattened popcorn box Frisbee-like through the air, its shadow flitting across the giant screen.

I had witnessed misguided youths engaging in such sordid activities and had whispered a silent prayer for their souls. For if they were apprehended, the secret room would echo with their screams, deadened by the noise of the popcorn maker. I had merely been talking, laughing, disturbing those around me. Not so bad. And yet . . .

"But . . ." I stammered.

"No 'buts.' Be quiet and get out here."

I stumbled over Tommy's feet and looked down at him. His eyes said it all. Tear-rimmed, they were gazing at his big brother's face for the last time.

"But, I wasn't . . ." I protested.

"What'd I say? Shut up and move it." Brandishing his flashlight, he gave me a not-so-gentle push up the aisle.

I turned to plead my case one more time, and the flashlight's metal handle cracked sharply on my right elbow. "Owwww . . . my pitching arm."

"I don't wanna hear it. Keep moving."

And so, humiliated, I marched in time, much like the ragged Rangers trying to keep ahead of the French. It strengthened my fast-beating heart to know, however, that I did not march alone. Surrounding me, sitting in soft chairs, were my comrades. And they, with fierce resolve, would soon rise as one to overthrow this teenage tyrant. Come forward, stout hearts. Throw off your shackles. Save me 'fore I am devoured. Holy St. Peter, I was delirious.

Near the back, I heard some of my school friends giggle as I slumped past. "Look, they got Mike."

Through the swinging doors. Into the brightly lit lobby. Time was racing now. Perhaps I could make a run for it.

Suddenly, I felt the cold hand of death clutch my shirt collar. "This way," usher boy hissed. Steering my shaking body, he directed me toward the pop machine. "Sit your fat ass down here."

Collapsing onto a nearby bench, I faced my accuser in the light of day. Egad. With black hair greased back and upper lip curled in a sneer, he resembled Elvis. But Elvis didn't have a chipped front tooth and a hundred and eighty-four pimples. I thought I might hurl.

"Here's the deal, kid," he growled, poking me with the flashlight. "You're gonna sit right here until the movie ends, got it? You're not gonna walk around or go to the restroom or try to sneak back in. And if you talk to anyone, I'm gonna cut your tongue out."

Swooning in a near faint, I nodded in silent agreement.

Satan gave me one last satisfied scowl and slinked back into the darkened arena.

Well, not too much to do here. Rubbing my bruised elbow, I contemplated the rug's amoeba-like pattern for the next five minutes. The hum of the pop machine droned in my ear.

"Hey, Mike." Tommy's disembodied head materialized in the crack between the massive doors. Was it being held by the insane soldier? By the zit-faced usher? "Are you okay?"

And so, as frame after frame chattered through the projector in the tiny room above the audience, and hot popcorn exploded against the glass walls of the yellow-tinted machine in the lobby, Tommy kept me mute company during my imprisonment. It was a brother thing.

CHAPTER 9

"AND THE MOON IS FULL AND BRIGHT"

My father's bulky frame backed down the ladder step by step. First, his legs appeared through the attic's trap door, then his torso, head, and arms. Balanced above him was the treasure chest we longed to unearth annually in mid-October: the Halloween trunk. He plunked it down in the middle of our bedroom floor. "Go to it, guys."

Like gravediggers, Tommy and I disemboweled the stuffy coffin. Masks, hats, canes, wigs, wax teeth, plastic lanterns, rubber knives and clubs. Precious remnants from years past. Laughing, we tried on bits and pieces of former costumes: Tommy's clown wig, my Lone Ranger hat and mask, and—the scariest item—a Cubs cap and jacket.

As joyful as reminiscing was, it was just a warm-up for the main event, finding the perfect costume for this year. Johnny decided early on that he would be Dracula, so he purchased a black cape with red lining to complement wax vampire teeth and a tube of fake blood to drip down from the corners of his mouth. Cool.

Tommy opted for the Wolf Man. Shattering his piggy bank allowed him to buy an ultra-frightening wolf's mask with pointed ears, bleach-white teeth, and gleaming red eyes. He tested its fright factor on me early one Saturday morning as I lay half-asleep in my bed, facing the wall. Hearing low breathing in my ear, I raised my head to stare into Wolfie's face inches from my nose. My scream nearly raised the dead. Clearly inspired, Tommy lay in bed at night looking out the window and softly chanting:

"Even a man who's pure at heart,
Who says his prayers by night,
May become a wolf,
When the wolfsbane blooms,
And the moon is full and bright"

Little moron. I'd get even, assuming I found a suitable costume.

Halloween was now only ten days away. I scoured local magic shops searching for a disguise. Naturally, there was pressure to complete the troika and don a Frankenstein mask, a shabby old coat, torn jeans, and clunky boots. But I was stubborn in my desire for a unique personality. I argued that there were already too many of the good doctor's creations walking the suburban sidewalks and, furthermore, the big boots would slow me down in our ultimate quest: to cover as much territory and take in as much candy as possible before the nine o'clock curfew. The boys saw the wisdom in these words.

With not a day to lose, the answer came in the form of a horror magazine. This publication was devoted to behind-the-scenes stories of the making of monster movies, from costumes and make-up to settings and special effects.

Toward the back of the book were advertisements for everything a twisted ten-year-old boy could ever want. There, in the middle of the page, staring out at me, sat the spectre of death itself. The rubber mask was green in color with black, stringy hair. One side of the face had been burned or scarred—hopefully both—and was mottled in red and black. One protruding eyeball was yellow; the other was gone, a small slit in its place. Simply put, it was the most terrifying this-damn-face-is-going-to-scare-the-crap-out-of-you mask I had ever seen in my life. And this was only a picture.

The ad promised delivery within one week, barely enough time for its arrival. If it didn't come by then, I'd be forced to use a cork and a match with basic hobo attire. But it was a chance I was prepared to take, so I sent in my money with the order form. God speed the mail!

Meanwhile, strategic sessions were held. A battlefield map was created laying out our zigzag plan of attack to conquer the neighborhood. Each block was a choreographed series of arrows with corresponding time estimates for a range of six to eight streets in every direction, save to the south where the railroad tracks sat, an impenetrable blockade to the other side of town.

"Listen to me!" I shouted at the others. "This little trip you've planned all the way to Oak Avenue will never work. It's one street too many. We've got to start heading back at Elm Street or our bags will be full."

Terror gripped our group. Nothing could be more fatal to our objective than wasting precious time walking home to empty our pillowcases without being able to stop at more houses on the return trip.

"You're right," conceded Johnny, shaken by the near blunder. "We'll have to start back home when we reach Elm."

Adjustments were made, routes altered; every second counted. Subtle variations could be made during the siege. For example, if a neighbor gave out the large size Hershey or Milky Way, that house would be hit a second time later that night on an elaborate crisscross pattern to another sector. Conversely, if a cheapskate passed out orange and black no-name taffy, his house would be "tricked" near the end of the battle.

"What about Howie's?" asked Tommy.

"I dunno," I cringed.

Howie was a grown man with a wife and three small children. His house backed up to Johnny's. It was in his bushes that I'd buried myself the summer night Mr. Connor had tried to kill us. His annual treat was above and beyond the Butterfinger or Baby Ruth, more delectable than the Nestle Crunch or the Hershey with Almonds. Astonishing to all, he set up a grill in his garage and cooked hot dogs, the savory smell drifting out into the chill night air, beckoning hungry kids from blocks away.

"I'll tell you one thing," I continued. "Whenever it is we stop there, we're not taking any shortcuts." This was a veiled reference to two years ago when I had stepped on a ball and sprained my ankle while cutting through Howie's yard in the dark. The rest of the night was a disaster as I struggled along three or four houses behind my so-called friends in a vain attempt to keep pace. Eventually abandoning the chase, I broke down crying and hobbled home.

Looking back, that was par. I contracted the mumps in fourth grade and, rigid and swollen-faced, rested on the couch while Tommy and Johnny dumped their chocolate treasures in heaping piles on the living room floor. Second grade found me hunkered over the toilet with the stomach flu. And in first grade, it rained so hard that our drenched bodies were dragged in before dark. Come to think of it, this would be my first real Halloween since kindergarten, and I was going to live every minute of it.

Not a moment too soon, the greatest-ever horror mask arrived on the thirtieth. I was ready to roll.

Halloween broke bright and sunny; no rain was in the forecast. School provided a prelude to the madness of trick or treat. An all-school parade. Moms lined the route to take snapshots of their little dragons, mermaids, ladybugs, and fairy princesses. A "Best Costume" award, judged by the K-5 teachers, was presented to one lucky kid in each class. The fifth grade honor went to Doug. No surprise there. His wooden pirate's leg looked frighteningly real, and his "Aaaaargh, Matey!" sounded convincing as well.

The class party that followed the parade was a mixture of macabre and madcap. All the boys checked out Sylvia Rothman's Little Red Riding Hood costume and then swapped melted vanilla ice cream cups for packages of Jumbo Jawbreakers. At exactly 3:30, sugar coursing through our veins, we were released into the general population, the neat rows of homes awaiting the onslaught.

Following a quick bathroom break and a "Be home for dinner at five" command, Tommy and I broke free and crossed the street. Phase I of the campaign would begin with a blitzkrieg toward the highway. Count Dracula met us at the corner.

"Hey," I teased, my voice muffled by my mask, "you can't be outside yet. The sun's still up."

"Neither can he," countered Johnny, pointing at Wolf Man. "Not until the moon is full and bright."

"I'll show you a full moon."

Before Tommy could drop his pants, I cut him off. "Look, monster mates, there's no time for this bullshit. Let's get moving."

Just past Johnny's house, we bounded up the steps to the front porch of Mrs. Olson. She and Mr. Olson were recent immigrants from Sweden, unusual for the mostly Irish-Polish-Italian neighborhood. Also odd, they had no offspring, not even a dog. Ringing the doorbell twice in succession, we waited with growing impatience. Shadows on the sunlit front yard were lengthening.

We visualized Mrs. Olson heaving her tired butt off the couch. Then the shuffle across the worn, rose-patterned carpet. The click of the lock. The pulling back on the heavy oaken door.

"Trick or Treat!"

"Oh," she exclaimed, slapping her hands against the sides of her face, "is it dat time of year again?"

Oh, my Lord, I thought. She doesn't know what day it is. Having arrived in America the summer before last, she had experienced only one Halloween and simply hadn't placed any significance on the thirty-first of October. Instantly, I knew what this meant. Her modest brick ranch wasn't brimming over with bags of candy. She could probably smooth-talk her way out of it with the younger kids, but what about the older ones? They came after dark; they wore leather jackets with chains; they carried switchblades. And these weren't costumes. Why, they'd cut her into little pieces.

"Look, ma'am, it's okay . . ." I began.

"Vait," she said. "I vill be right back." She moved off into the recesses of the darkened living room until she vanished from view.

"What're we gonna do?" pleaded Johnny. "We can't wait all day for her to find some moldy candy in her pantry. We're wasting valuable time."

"He's right," added Tommy. "Let's leave."

"All right, I suppose we'd . . . wait, here she comes."

Mrs. Olson returned with her arms full. She proceeded to give each of us an apple, a nickel, and one quarter of a box of neatly wrapped Graham Crackers. If she kept up this pace, she'd be handing out cans of ravioli by evening.

"But," she stammered in broken English, "is dat enough?"

Well, I thought, there is that nice little TV in the corner. Do you think you could have it delivered to my bedroom by tomorrow? Instead, I mumbled, "Yeah, sure, that's enough. Thanks."

As we left satisfied, I wondered what tonight's thugs would do to her. "Sure, lady, we'll be happy to take your quarters, won't we, boys? And your dollar bills too. Ha. Ha. Ha."

Our map served us well. Up and down block after block, like Marines on a mission. We were close to home when our sacks became heavy, a crucial strategy for success. As daylight faded into dark, we charged up the front porch steps. Our weary mom, ladle in hand, was juggling preparing dinner with handing out treats. We waved a quick hello to her and headed for the bedroom.

"Mom," I yelled, yanking off my sweat-soaked mask, "can Johnny stay for dinner?"

"If it's all right with his mom. Does he like spaghetti?"

"Do you like spaghetti?"

He nodded.

"Yeah, he likes it!"

Tommy and I unceremoniously dumped our candy onto the rug—on our own sides of the room. Then came the real ritual of Halloween: inspecting one's stash. A quick overview committed to memory the number of decent candy bars, like gold nuggets to prospectors. A more thorough tooth-combing revealed hidden gems: a package of Whoppers Malted Milk Balls, the square, silver shine of a Chunky ("What-a-chunk-a-chocolate"), and—the most sought after—a Tootsie Roll Pop.

There were bad surprises as well. We both found orange and black hard taffy, the kind that pulled out fillings. Johnny reached into his sack and held up some bright orange circus peanuts. "Who gave out this crap? We've got to go back and trick 'em." Necco Wafers were a mixed blessing. The thin, chalk-like candy was only half bad. Brown ones = chocolate delight; pink ones = Pepto-Bismol flavor.

"Ha!" Tommy shrieked. His fist, raised in triumph, clutched a multi-colored cellophane package. "I got Chuckles!"

We had been to the same houses. I should have them too. Frantic, I clawed through the candy. With an exclamation of pure relief, I pulled my own package from the bottom of the pile. "Ah, ha!"

"I'll trade my yellow and black for your red," Tommy suggested slyly.

"Do I look stupid?" Basic kid rule: never give up the cherry-flavored anything.

The real bartering would begin later that night when the mountains of candy rose shin-high from the floor.

"I'm going to take a whiz," I stated. "So help me, there better be nothin' missing when I get back. But just to make sure . . ." Sneering, I snatched both Butterfingers and shoved them into my pocket.

After a hurried dinner, we rushed out into the now cold October night. It was only six o'clock. Three hours to go. Along the way, we bumped into friends, advanced scouts on the prairie eager to share tips.

"Mrs. Hulbert on Birch is giving out Snickers," and "Old Lady Crenshaw over by the school has got fresh popcorn—it's good."

Of course, there were also negative reports, most of them urban legends. "Old Man McGuire is passing out apples. Don't take them. Sandy Wilkens said Frankie Green bit into one, and there was a razor blade inside." Yeah, sure, I thought, and Mr. Santelli, an amateur magician who lived near the ball field, put spells on kids that caused them to grow up to be servants of Satan.

The next few hours dizzy-danced along. And then, toward the end of the long night, our sacks straining from the glorious weight, fate intervened. An accidental rendezvous with Bobby, Jimmy, Eddie, and Greg set the stage for an explosive finale to All Hallow's Eve. First came small talk and exaggerated inventory—"That's nothing. I've got at least twenty Clark bars in my pile at home!" Then, Bobby reached deliberately into the pocket of his disheveled hobo pants. Grinning, he produced a small, round, red object. Had he pulled out a .357 Magnum, we couldn't have been more surprised.

"Oh, brother!" I exclaimed in delirious disbelief.

"What is it?" asked Tommy.

"What is it?" mocked Bobby. "Why, don't you know? It's a cherry bomb."

"Where d'ja get it?" stammered Johnny, knowing full well that the fine state of Illinois did not sell or allow such firepower. And most likely for this very reason: to keep it out of the hands of moronic juveniles like us.

"My dad picked it up on our vacation down South."

Of course, I reflected. The South, still hoping to refight the Civil War, was stocking up on ammo.

"Did you steal it from him?" Jimmy, dressed as Zorro, was visibly excited at the thought of blowing something up.

"No. He gave it to me. But he said to be careful and only shoot it off in an open field."

"So what're we gonna do with it?" drooled Jimmy.

Suggestions were advanced, considered, rejected.

"No, Jimmy," said Bobby. "Mrs. Daulton's cat won't stand still long enough for that."

"Well, it's better than Eddie's idea." Eddie's proposal involved revenge on Mr. Connor.

"Didn't you learn your lesson that night?" I asked, remembering with restrained glee how we had turned Eddie and Jimmy into sacrificial lambs.

"I told you. I wasn't even there."

Greg wanted to drop it lit into a little kid's trick or treat bag, but the mere thought of destroying candy was anathema to us.

Suddenly, I blurted out, "Why don't we go over to Mary Linder's house and blow up her Jack-O-Lantern?"

Eddie stared at me through his WWII fighter pilot goggles. "You're in love with her, aren't you?"

That was it, of course. And now everyone knew it. Why else would I have proposed this violent act? When a ten-year-old boy suffers from unrequited love, he will do anything to get the girl's attention. What more creative way than to blow her pumpkin art to smithereens in her own front yard? Now, there's an act of desperation.

"No," I said through clenched teeth. "I just think it would be fun."

"Let's do it!" yelled Bobby. And we were off.

Seven friends, hearts beating fast, paused in the relative safety of the far side of the street. This would be tough. The target sat glowing on an outdoor windowsill directly beside the porch leading to the front door. To retrieve it, one of us was going to have to crawl up to it and pluck it from its perch without being spotted by someone from inside the house. Greg, ironically decked out in army fatigues, was chosen for his alert, cat-like nature.

Silently, swiftly, as if crossing an expansive, moonlit field to a beckoning foxhole, Greg snaked his way across the street to the shadows of the neatly trimmed hedge that bordered the walkway. From there, partially concealed, he belly-crawled ever closer to his lifeless prey. We held our collective breaths as he suddenly stood, reached up, and seized it with both hands. Cradling it like a football under one arm, he ran back to the hedge.

"Stay here," I commanded, handing my sack of treats to Tommy. "We don't need everyone. Bobby and I'll go."

"Keep a lookout for trouble," Bobby added.

We met Greg in the front yard near the main sidewalk. Handing the pumpkin off quarterback style to Bobby, he bolted past us and across the street to join the others. The two of us, needles of apprehension pricking our necks, knelt down on the hard lawn and carefully positioned the cherry bomb between Jack's teeth. Stifling laughs, we bent forward. Bobby had two matches. He lit one, but the breeze snuffed it out before he could touch it to the wick. We rolled our eyes at one another. The second match was handled with more fragility. Cupping our last hope between his hands and shielding it from the wind, Bobby struck it on the sidewalk and pressed it against the tip of the wax-coated cord. Until my dying day, I swear we heard the sibilant sound of the ignited wick.

We ran like the Hounds of Hell were on our heels. The others—cowards, the lot of them—had fled with the first match spark, and we finally caught up to them at the intersection, where we waited for the blast. It never came.

"Damn it!" said Bobby angrily.

"What happened? I heard it light," I wailed. "At least I think I did."

After much heated deliberation, we realized we had to go back. This was no time to abort the mission.

"C'mon," I said, grabbing Bobby's arm.

"It's no use. I'm outta matches."

"We'll use the candle." This had become a labor of love. "I'll light it this time."

We marched with firm resolve toward the flicker of Jack's soft glow like condemned men marching toward the dim light of the execution chamber. We might die, but our fate would be played out with nobility and courage.

As we stared into Jack's taunting gaze, our faces only inches from the bomb, it was clear that a very short wick was all that remained. I clutched my mask in my left hand, took a deep breath, and, my right hand shaking, stretched the candle out and touched its flame to the stub. Sssssssssssss . . .

We had plenty of time. To stand and turn. The explosion from behind rocked our ears. Like frightened rabbits, we bounded forward, chunks of bright orange shrapnel whizzing past our heads. One large fragment nailed Bobby in the back. "Uuuh," he moaned. Another gooey lump of Jack's insides splattered against the back of my neck and oozed down into my collar. "Our Father, who art in Heaven . . ."

In the category of lessons learned, this little incident would forevermore top the list. To be so stupid as to have placed my young face next to a cherry bomb—albeit for love's sake—was tantamount to insanity. Was it possible that I was born without a brain? For weeks after, I shuddered whenever I thought about how Bobby and I had narrowly escaped being blinded for life or worse—an untimely visit from Dr. Death. On the brighter side, the Butterfingers tasted especially good that year.

Chapter 10

"Oscar"

Oscar Melillo was a real person. You can look it up. According to the *Baseball Encyclopedia*, he played second base and hit .260 over twelve seasons in the Major Leagues, mostly for the hapless St. Louis Browns. My brother and I had heard of his exploits often, but we had never met him, even though he was my dad's cousin twice removed, or something. That all changed when my grandma died.

My father's immigrant mother had lived in a rambling old house on the North Side of Chicago for as long as I had known her. Her husband—my grandfather—had been a coal miner in Pennsylvania who had died before I was born. Whenever we visited her, we explored the cavernous upper floor of the house, where mysterious trunks hid under rainbow-colored quilts, and the tomb-like basement, with its "secret" exit leading up five concrete steps to paint-chipped, hinged doors.

The main floor of the house was where she lived, sleeping on a sofa in the living room. Keeping her company was Boo-chee-ka-boo-chee, her songbird, whom she conversed with only in Italian. To amuse us, she would let him out of his cage to fly around the room, chirping brightly. Once, he pooped on her shoulder, and she swore at him. But she loved the bird, her only companion.

A freeze-frame of her life would reveal: summer picnics in the forest preserve sitting in a folding chair slurping Popsicles and shouting out encouragement to my father and his brothers playing softball; cold winter nights bundled in a flowered robe, hunched over a table, skillfully setting the final jigsaw piece into place; lonely days delicately sewing monograms onto handkerchiefs to be given to her grandchildren as birthday or Christmas gifts.

But she had not always been so white and withered. My father told us how she had saved her sons one day in the small house in Pennsylvania. The boys were playing in their unheated bedroom one morning when a shuffling noise drew them to their closet. Carefully opening the door, they froze in horror. A large diamondback rattle-snake was comfortably coiled on a bundle of linen. Before it could strike, the boys' frightened cries brought my grandma running. Bursting in like Batman, broom in hand, she attacked. Propelled downward by her massive arms, the broom landed blow after blow on the bewildered reptile. By the end of the carnage, its nearly lifeless body bounced again and again across the wooden floor. In a final Godfather-like act of brutality, she shouted "morire" and crushed its bloated head with the heel of her brogans.

The night she died, my father left to visit her in the hospital and didn't return until morning. At eighty, complications from diabetes had taken her.

Arrangements were made. Tommy and I missed school to get haircuts. Slicked up, we wore jackets and thin, black ties to the wake, which lasted three long nights. Mom instructed us how to behave, what to say and do; yes, our cousins would be there, but we were not to laugh or joke around or disturb adults with needless questions. We were to sit quietly in our chairs, speak politely to relatives we had never met before, and pray devoutly along with the priest.

In spite of my mom's good intentions, nothing could have prepared us for the sight of Grandma in a brand new dress—we had never seen her in one—wrinkled hands folded over a crucifix, eyes closed as if she was asleep, and lying in a shiny black box with gold handles. I had never seen a dead person before, and I was awestruck. My father went up first; he hugged my uncle briefly and then knelt at the casket. When he stood again, he beckoned us to come forward. Mom's hands gently touched our backs and, in a trance, we inched forward.

When we reached the coffin, which was surrounded by fragrant flowers, my dad smiled softly as if to tell us it was all right. We knelt down, and he placed a strong hand on each of our shoulders. "Say a prayer," he whispered.

This was a good idea; one prays with eyes closed. I squeezed them shut, so as not to have to look at Grandma's face, and pretended to pray. I was actually thinking about her, about life and death, about God and Heaven. Obvious questions burned through my mind, but no answers came. When I finally opened my eyes, I nearly fainted. A picture of me stared out from the coffin's inner lid. Similar shots of Tommy and Linda were next to mine. Mom had put them there while I was wandering in thought. "Spooked out" didn't begin to cover it.

"Mom," I whispered, "why is my picture in there?"

"Shhh. I'll explain later."

Back in our folding chairs, my mom told us that these photos were to comfort Grandma in the afterlife. Some comfort, I thought. "And this, Saint Peter, is my grandson Mike. Doesn't his cowlick remind you of Alfalfa?"

Good Lord, wakes were odd.

For the next three hours, the old folks came. They wept, laughed, and remembered. There was an occasional, awkward introduction—"Are these your boys, Hank? Why, the last time I saw them, they were this high." But for the most part, we were ignored. Our weird cousin Theodore offered me a nickel if I went up to the casket and touched Grandma's hand to see if it was cold. Ignoring decorum, I flicked his balls and walked away.

On the second night, Tommy and I asked if we could stay home and help the babysitter with Linda. My mother's answer was a firm "no." She did, however, take pity on us at the wake by allowing us to walk with our cousin

Kenny to a pantry next door. We bought some candy and stepped out into the parking lot. Free at last from the stifling confines of the funeral parlor, we huddled against the November chill and shot the shit. Kenny, an only child, went to a Catholic school and fascinated us with stories of the nuns and their obsession with violence.

"And another time, Sister Mary Ignacious split Vito Antonelli's knuckles to the bone with a metal ruler. There was blood everywhere. He's crying, and she sends him to the bathroom to wash the blood off. And just last week, Laura McGinn talked during math, and Sister taped her mouth shut by wrapping it all around her head and sent her home like that. She looked like a damn mummy. The next day, she comes to school, and her hair's all cut off, real short. Her mom had to do that to get the tape off."

My father had once said that he wanted us to go to public schools so that we'd grow up normal. Listening to Kenny's horror stories, I silently thanked Dad for his wisdom. And then, out of the blue, our cousin nonchalantly dropped the bombshell. "I hear old Oscar's comin' tomorrow night."

"What? Oscar? Oscar Melillo? Coming here?"

At last. Our distant relative. A former Major Leaguer. And we, in all our puny insignificance, were going to meet him.

Would we prove worthy?

The next night, my dad forbade us to bring gloves, bats, or balls to be autographed. He issued a stern reminder to us regarding the purpose of the wake, and then rather reluctantly agreed to introduce us to "Mr. Melillo."

"Did he really play against the Babe?" Tommy asked, his face a mask of wonder.

"I'll let you ask him that."

We didn't even notice him when he walked into the parlor. Short, silver-haired, and wearing a dark brown suit, he blended in with the other ancients. We had never considered that he might be old. After all, he had been a baseball player.

"Dad," I asked impatiently, "when's he coming?"

My father smiled. "He's been in the room for fifteen minutes."

"What? Where?"

"Over there. By the door."

When I at last figured out which person my dad was referring to, a wave of disappointment washed over me. "But that guy's old."

"He wasn't always."

True. But, as he lifted a wrinkled hand to acknowledge my father from a distance, I had trouble visualizing him as the middleman in a bag-scraping, dirt-flying, spikes-slashing double play. Permanently bent over, he limped toward us, a cane bracing him as he walked.

"Manners," cautioned my father.

"Henry," he said, his voice like tires on gravel, "I'm sorry about your mom."

"Thank you, Oscar."

After adult talk, my dad turned to us. "Oscar, these are my sons, Mike and Tom. Boys, this is Mr. Melillo."

Eyes glinting, he smiled at us. "What good-looking young men. I'm sorry about your grandma. She was a wonderful woman. I'm sure you miss her already."

"Yes, sir. Thank you, sir," we mumbled in unison.

"So, are you boys ball players?"

"Yes, sir." Could he tell just by looking at us?

"I played ball once upon a time."

Tommy, always less timid, blurted out, "Tell us about it, please, sir."

The dam burst. For the next thirty or so minutes, Oscar Melillo, former professional baseball player and our blood relative, told us about his past. And a glorious past it had been, filled with bean balls and squeeze bunts, doubles off the wall and triples in the corner, double-headers in the fiery heat of the day and card games on lonesome trains rattling to somewhere in the middle of the night.

"What was Babe Ruth like?"

"The Bambino." It was not a question. Rather, a statement. A name, softly spoken with respect by one who had witnessed his feats up close and personal. "Why, when the Babe popped one up, we'd get dizzy waiting for it to come down."

We laughed.

"That's enough, boys." My father's subdued voice broke into our once-in-a-lifetime fantasy. "The priest is here."

For what-seemed-like-forever-and-probably-was, we knelt and prayed. Our clasped fingers ached; our knees became numb. I knew I was supposed to be concentrating on the prayers, but my mind kept flashing back to Oscar's stories. At one point, he had lifted up his pants cuff a little to scratch his leg.

"What are those?" I had asked, bewildered.

"Spikes. I was a second baseman, you know."

Thinking back on the sight of Oscar's bony leg with its innumerable scars, I knew then, for the first time in my young life, that I didn't have what it took to be a professional baseball player. To compete like Oscar had. To stand in, foot on the bag, fear in his eyes but courage in his heart as he released the throw inches above the sliding runner's head to complete the double play. And if a thousand opponents cut his legs to ribbons over his long career, then he wore the marks with pride because he had faced his fear and conquered it.

Suddenly, another image seared my overloaded brain. It was Grandma, cursing in Italian, beating the life out of a deadly viper. But I saw something else as well. I saw fear in her eyes. The fear of an immigrant woman whose husband went bravely into the mines every day because they both wanted a better life for their children. And I understood that people did what they must to survive, to move on through life with courage and dignity. Grandma may have been gone, and Oscar may have been just-another-unremarkable-old-man-come-to-pay-his-respects, but they could teach a ten-year-old boy volumes about what it meant to live a purposeful life.

When the priest concluded an eternity later, I rose stiffly, staring at Grandma, who was now at peace. She had raised my father and his siblings and sent them out into the world. My father had grown up to fight in the Battle of the Bulge, learn a trade, and was now, with my mom, raising three children of his own, an admirable task considering how much we had yet to learn.

Fighting back a healthy dose of guilt, I looked hurriedly around the room. I wanted to thank Mr. Melillo for spending time and sharing stories with us about a small part of his life. But he was gone. He hadn't even said good-bye.

A couple of days after Grandma's funeral, Tommy and I were getting ready for school. The first day we had gone back, we had told schoolmates about meeting Oscar, but they had never heard of him and didn't believe us.

Dad, leaving for work, poked his head in our bedroom door. "Hey, guys, I forgot something. I've had a lot on my mind the past few days."

In his hand were two torn scraps of paper, one for each of us. "Mr. Melillo wanted you to have these."

We reached out with trembling hands to grasp the identical pieces of paper.

"Don't lose them. They may be valuable someday. See ya tonight."

Tommy and I stared at the scribbled script before us. In bold, black writing, the name stood out: *Oscar Melillo*. He hadn't forgotten to say good-bye after all.

CHAPTER 11

"SKUNKY SPUNKY"

My cousin Kenny and I stealthily approached the creek's bank, crunching carefully through the dry leaves and twigs. With every third or fourth step, we stopped to listen. Hearing only the muttering of water as it slid over rocks, we resumed the hunt. We moved slowly. Convinced there were pheasants up ahead, we squeezed our shotguns ever tighter. We could no longer see my dad and uncle, but we knew where they were, flanking our right side at the top of the ravine, waiting for us to flush a bird.

Back then, the sight of two young boys carrying shotguns in a wooded suburb did not bring a phalanx of police with weapons, dogs, and bullhorns: "Drop your guns, and raise your arms above your heads where we can see them! Now, fall on the ground! Place your hands behind your backs! One false move and we shoot to kill!" A friendly wave and "hello" from a passing cop was more likely. Hunting was a common practice in the woods and cornfields all over the Chicago area. One didn't have to drive for hours to find a good spot.

The first time I went out—at age eight—I carried only a BB gun. The flapping of the pheasant's wings as he rose up and flew low above the corn, followed closely by the roar of my father's shotgun, scared me half to death. The bird landed hard—my dad seldom missed—crashing down through the crisp stalks to the dirt below. We hustled over to the beautiful, blood-soaked body. Not yet dead, it panted for air. My father reached down quickly, twisted its colorful neck, and it was over. Feeling natural pity for one of God's creatures, I refused to lift it off the ground. Dad carried it back to the car. His philosophy was simple: killing the birds was okay as long as you ate them. "It's just like chicken or turkey, only someone else kills those for us."

After lunch, I aimed a shotgun for the first time in my life. Not at a moving target but at a bottle sitting on a stump.

"Remember," Dad cautioned, "keep the stock pressed tightly against your shoulder."

"Why?"

"You'll see."

I saw. The kick from the 12-gauge nearly knocked me to the ground. What, I thought, was the purpose of this? Couldn't we be a fishing family?

Now, two years later, I had my own gun and a lust for blood. Every Saturday in season, we hunted. Our most frequented farm was located off US Route 30 a half hour out of Aurora. Weather was never an issue. My dad, having liberated Europe, showed extreme displeasure if I suggested that it was too cold-snowy-rainy-sleety to hunt. Encased in hats with earflaps and wearing thick gloves, marching drearily like war-weary soldiers, Kenny and I scanned the horizon only to see my dad out in front. With an infantryman's cadence, he moved swiftly across the frozen field. Chin held high, unshaven face jutting out against the whipping wind, shoulders gathering stripes of snow, he surveyed with squinting eyes of steel the battlefield looming ahead of him. A wave of his burly arm signaled to the troops to close ranks, don't lag behind, the enemy was near. Occasionally, sensing prey hidden in the high grass, a Patton-proud smile would crease his chapped lips. Whenever I saw that malevolent grin, I knew some poor pheasant's time on earth was short.

Our party lacked only one necessity: a good hunting dog. Kenny surprised us once by bringing along his neighbor's dog, a "mix" of questionable breeding named Spunky. This shaggy, black mutt was focused more on bounding playfully through the dry grass and chasing rabbits up and down the rows of corn than he was on cornering helpless birds. By mid-morning, my father and uncle were frustrated with Spunky's lack of discipline. Our laughter at his most recent escapade, chasing a frightened squirrel up a tree, didn't help matters. But the day's light mood suddenly turned serious.

We were halfway through a pass between the rows of corn, the amber stalks rustling in the gentle breeze. Suddenly, a commotion ahead. Startled, I charged forward to spot Spunky's legs sticking out of a hole in the ground. Inside, a ferocious fight took place. What was this stupid dog up to? Was he mauling a bunny rabbit?

As I watched in suspended horror, all sound ceased, and Spunky-the-dog-warrior dragged a bloodied carcass up out of the ground. He did have a killer instinct after all, but what had he killed? It was way too big to be a rabbit. Then, the pungent odor, as sour as an outhouse on a hot summer's day, hit me.

"What happened?" yelled Kenny, clutching my shoulder from behind with a trembling hand.

"Your wonder dog killed a skunk."

The ride home was unspeakable. The wide-open windows had no effect at all. Mile after nauseating mile, we gagged through flannel sleeves pressed over our mouths and noses. My uncle said we should have shot Spunky, left him in the field, and told his owner that he ran after a pheasant and never came back.

"Or," I piped up, "we could let him out here and tell your neighbor that the skunk killed him."

A tomato juice bath in Kenny's garage healed the dog, but my dad's car had no such remedy. Thanks to good old Spunk, it stunk of skunk the entire winter. My mother, I believe, contemplated divorce. My father just fumed.

Thanksgiving broke clear and cold. For every year of my life, my family had celebrated the holiday at home with my maternal grandparents. So, even before I rolled out of bed, my nostrils took in the rich aroma of the turkey cooking in the oven.

Tradition was the order of the day. View the Macy's parade from New York. Watch a bit of the annual NFL game from Detroit. Toss around a football in the yard. Grandpa was a favorite of mine. He had arms of steel, formed over years of cutting stone for a living. With a Chesterfield between his lips and a sparkle in his eyes that belied his advancing age, he took an interest in our hobbies and activities. He had taken Tommy and me to our first-ever Cubs game at Wrigley Field, and he always thumbed through our baseball cards and told us which players had been traded, always a revelation. He and Grandma, who was soft and pliable—an easy mark for any toys we wanted—lived in an apartment in Evanston. She worked nights for Ma Bell, and they spent most Sundays and every major holiday at our house.

By three o'clock, the table had been set with the fine china. The pilgrim and Indian wax candles surrounded the fall centerpiece, hand-crafted by my dad as a visual reminder that, before the War, he had been a florist. Soon after, the serving plates and bowls, heaping with steaming mounds of white and dark turkey, stuffing, soft rolls, corn, beans, and two kinds of potatoes—mashed and sweet—were passed around. The obligatory Jell-O mold was the last to circle the table. We were poised to pig out.

"Who's going to pray?" Mom asked.

Grandpa volunteered. He prayed for the usual things: family, health, safety, and peace on earth. He also prayed for our new president—"Thank you, Lord, for helping the people come to their senses and elect a Democrat"—and the outcome of the recent World Series—"And we are especially thankful that the Yankees lost for a change."

"Amen."

Two bites later, Grandma sighed loudly and said she was full. Everyone laughed. This, too, was a family tradition. For the next hour, stories filled the air. These were the times when, as children, we listened more than we talked for a change and were rewarded with snapshots from the past.

"... and your father was hunting, of course, and so Grandpa and I had to open the flower shop. But we forgot the keys. So Grandpa had to climb through the transom. That's when he fell and broke his ankle."

"... we were just coming out of church—a beautiful morning it was—and Father O'Reilly walked right up to us and blurted out that the Japs had bombed Pearl Harbor. That's how we found out."

"... no, that was Uncle Huey. And he wasn't a pirate. He just had a wooden leg."

"... hands down, your father had the hottest car at Evanston High."

"... that's when Grandpa learned once and for all not to throw rocks at a hornet's nest. His face was swollen for days."

"... and just when we reached the top, the Pair-O-Chutes stopped, and there we were for about an hour. I almost died of fright."

And on and on and on. Our elders abandoned their roles and became children again, or young singles, or newlyweds—everyday people leading everyday lives with hopes and dreams and faults and frailties. I pictured my parents staring at my father's draft notice and realizing that their plans for a family would have to be put on hold. I saw my grandfather as a golden-haired boy standing in a shallow Iowa stream and hooking a catfish on his line. And these mental images amazed me. It slowly sunk in that this bond of family was what we were to be thankful for, then and in the years to come.

The pumpkin pie, smothered in an obscene amount of whipped cream, was forced down our gullets—mincemeat pie was my dad's annual fixation—and the repast was over. Everyone pitched in to wash and dry the dishes, and the family retired to the living room. I lay on my back, my bloated stomach extending above me, and watched through the window as the sun made its rapid descent. The rays reflected off the rectangular mirror and splashed across the front of the TV, giving color to the black and white picture. I embraced the warmth of our home, and I was thankful. How could it have been otherwise?

PART III
WINTER/SPRING

CHAPTER 12

"YOU BETTER WATCH OUT"

The coming of Christmas in our lives was always signaled by two events, both in early December. The first was the putting up of the outdoor decorations. I usually helped my father by feeding him the strings of red-green-blue-yellow big-bulb lights. He would perch atop the ladder in the sometimes-bitter-cold air and tack the strings into the white wood along two sides of the corner ranch. Next came more lights around the sole evergreen in front of the house. Finally, the giant, snow-topped, red bells were hung to frame the living room picture window, where the tree would sit. It looked classy—never overdone, never underdone. By contrast, Mr. Tripp across the street would open his front door, step onto his porch in his bathrobe and slippers, and fling a string of lights in the general direction of a clump of evergreens beneath his living room window. Wherever they landed is where they stayed. Some hung haphazardly off branches; others were burned out. Made us giddy with Christmas spirit.

The second major coming-of-Christmas event was a trip to the city to visit Marshall Field's. With its story-book window displays and its legendary Walnut Room, Field's defined the holiday for generations of Chicago families.

Santa was there, too, surrounded by fluffy cotton "snow" and demented-looking elves. It was a "must do" to wait in the endlessly weaving line, sit on his furry, germ-infested lap, and—after lying to his bearded face about how good we'd been all year—recite from memory a list of toys, games, and puzzles we more or less expected him to deliver on demand. Funny, we never once asked for the clothes we always received. Tommy and I knew, of course, the truth, the Santa myth having been exposed as soon as we started school years earlier. But we pretended for our little sister Linda as well as for our own self-interests.

Before the "North Pole" visit, however, we pushed-shoved-weaved our way into Field's famous toy department, where untold treasures awaited. It didn't take long to find Number One on my list: the Civil War set. It was not in a box. The crafty merchants had constructed a plaster of Paris battlefield and painted it to make it look realistic. On it rested the many pieces. There were the rubber molds—blue for the Union soldiers, gray for the Confederates, white for Lincoln, Grant, and Lee—and the plastic cannons and shell-marked bridges. There was the Southern mansion in colored tin, with ivy creeping up the red brick walls. There were brown charging horses and a green copse of trees. The soldiers were running, marching, kneeling, shooting, and being shot; some, along with their horses, lay mortally wounded, enhancing the realism. It was a violent, blood-soaked landscape that spoke of Bull Run, Shiloh, and Gettysburg, and it fueled my desire to re-create these famous battles on my bedroom floor.

I had spoken to my cousin Kenny the week before, and he was asking for the same set. The thought of combining the two for an afternoon of unadulterated warfare brought tears of joy to my eyes. I stood and gaped at the scene before me. My thoughts raced. Is-it-possible-this-could-be-mine-on-Christmas-day-am-I-worthy-have-I-been-good-enough? Wait! Have I? Have I been good enough?

My brother's whisper broke the silence. "I suppose if Dad finds out it was you who broke the Suttons' window with the football, you won't be playing with those figures anytime soon."

"Shut up."

"Well, it's just that I don't want you to end up with coal in your stocking."

This was a very real threat. Last Christmas, our weird cousin Theodore misbehaved one time too many when, stupidly, he had flushed an M-80 down the toilet to see what would happen. Uncle Lou made sure he received zero presents under the tree and a load of sticks, rocks, and fireplace ashes in his stocking. My dad remarked that this was a good lesson for boys who couldn't learn to "act right." I shivered at the thought.

"Okay," I relented, "what do you want?"

"Make my bed for two weeks." Tommy, the master blackmailer, was losing his touch. He could've gotten more.

"Fine."

He smiled and walked away, heading toward some cheap, battery-operated roller coaster.

Scowling at his back, I moved into the book section to see if a new Peanuts collection had been released. I had grown up following the antics of Charlie Brown, Lucy, Linus, Schroeder, Snoopy, and the gang. Somehow, it was comforting to know that there were kids in these strips we could relate to as they interacted with each other outside the world of adults. Already, Charlie Brown's dismal failures at kite flying, baseball, bowling, and the like had touched a nerve within me. We weren't all born to be standouts; it was okay to be normal. An "everyman" of sorts.

Later, we took Linda to see Santa, where she spat up on him until my dad pulled her off his lap. I stood beside him and asked politely for the Civil War set, a couple of books, and a Zorro watch. Now, if I could just survive three more weeks of volunteering to help Mom with the dishes, watching over my little sister and pretending I liked it, and not punching out Tommy just because it was fun, then I should get what I wanted most on Christmas morning.

A week before the blessed holiday, my family piled into the Buick and drove off in the dead of night to search for that most sacred of all symbols, a live Christmas tree. Artificial trees had recently come out—bright silver, put-together-from-the-bottom-up trees with revolving, colored gels. My father, always the innovator, made sure that we were the first ones on our block to own one. But that was last year's fashion. This year, he had an even more twisted idea about how to revitalize an old-fashioned, pine-scented, painstakingly-draped-with-tinsel, ornamented, lighted, star-on-the-top Christmas tree. The key word here was flock, and it was his new passion.

Flock was an appropriate word for the gooey-sticky-gloppy substance. Sprayed on, it clung paste-like to the branches of a tree. Its only more disgusting trait was its choice of colors: baby blue, pink, lavender, and a few other supposedly festive hues. Dad picked out a particularly dark shade of purple. Good God, I thought, we're going to be the laughingstock of the neighborhood. Cars will crowd our street at night to see what everyone's talking about, to point and make derisive comments. "Have you ever seen anything like that, Myrtle? The poor man must be color blind."

In the end, we picked out a stunningly beautiful tree. Not that it made a difference; it would be hidden beneath thick layers of purple slop. My father and grandfather would act as executioners. One mid-week evening, they dragged the tree to the basement, its perfumed boughs unaware of their fate: death by flocking. Wearing masks over their mouths, the King's men proceeded to turn on their instrument of torture, and the chamber filled with noxious fumes. My mom, brother, and I sat spellbound at the top of the stairs.

After the "whoosing" noise stopped, I heard my father say, "That looks good! Let's take 'er up!"

The next thing I knew, the two men were heaving the obscene purple object up the stairs. As they grunted their way up, blobs of flock splattered on the steps beneath their feet.

"Get the damn kids out of the way!"

My father seldom swore, reserving it for significant moments such as this one to reinforce exactly how tense-frustrated-angry he was. Perhaps inhaling the near-toxic blasts from the flock sprayer had tilted him toward madness. He certainly looked like it as he hurtled in our direction, eyes bulging and muscles straining, dragging the vandalized tree and my grandfather behind him.

Mom yanked on our arms to save us from the oncoming freight. Dad jerked the top half of the tree through the portal when it abruptly stopped; it was wedged tightly. Red faced and sweating, he yelled down to my grandfather, who was invisible beneath the behemoth. "Push, Grandpa! Push as hard as you can!"

A long thirty seconds later, the messy monster was born, squeezing through the opening with an explosion, leaving lichen-like velvet patches stuck on the door jamb. Grandpa appeared as well, his hands glued to the trunk."Turn it!" screamed Mom in wild-eyed fright. The men labored to steer through the kitchen, branches reaching out to scatter porcelain knickknacks off shelves.

"We're almost there!" my father shouted triumphantly, like Columbus approaching land. "I can see the living room!"

Cautiously, we followed the carnage through the kitchen and dining room until we could poke our heads around the corner and see Dad and Grandpa straining to lift the satanic beast onto its altar. When it was rammed home and tightened down, tilting only slightly, my father could only look up at it and smile. "Well, whad'ya think? It's a beauty, isn't it?"

We were speechless.

Christmas Eve arrived right on time, as it could be counted on to do. Some year, if it didn't make its appearance, little boys and girls around the world would be plunged into everlasting despair. We helped Mom decorate cookies—Santas, bells, trees, and stars—with colored icing. Nervous conversation accompanied the task.

"Do you think Santa will come?"

"Only if you've been good," reiterated Mom for the millionth time.

"Santa," cooed Linda with a smile, apparently forgetting that she had spat up on him only weeks earlier. In a twisted touch of irony, she would find a doll that peed waiting for her under the tree. Santa justice.

"Mom," I asked hesitantly, "do you think we can open just one present tonight before Mass?"

"Maybe. We'll ask your father when he gets home." Characteristic of their generation, Mom always deferred to Dad in everything. It was almost as if, in spite of the fact that she had grown up during the Depression and survived the War years alone while Dad was overseas, she still had to seek his approval for her decisions. I worried that our house might catch on fire someday, and she would say, "I'm not sure we should evacuate yet. Let's wait until your father comes home and ask him."

"Does Mike get extra presents again this year?" Tommy whined.

"Of course," said Mom, smiling angelically in my direction.

"Of course," I repeated, smiling sardonically in Tommy's direction.

The reason for this bounty was simple: my birthday fell on Christmas day. This year, I would be turning eleven. This fact, along with my first-born status, made me quite intolerable at this time of year. I was spoiled, and I knew it.

I wasn't supposed to be born on Christmas. Unusual for the first child, I was two weeks early. As my mom told it, she and my father had returned from midnight Mass, had busily prepared their apartment for a ten o'clock brunch with friends, and had settled down for what turned out to be a short winter's nap around three in the morning. Two hours later, she experienced the first salvo of labor pains. Waking my father with the traditional, "It's time"—to which he supposedly replied, "You're nuts; go back to sleep"—she convinced him to drive to Evanston Hospital. I was delivered at nine-thirty that Christmas morning while my dad made frenzied phone calls telling invited guests not to show up for the brunch, no one was home.

My embellished version of the "second miracle Christmas birth" was somewhat different. I liked to remember me popping out in the car—knowing full well there would be no room for us at the hospital—and saying my first words: "Merry Christmas! You didn't think you were going to keep me cooped up inside there all day, did you? Now, where are my presents?"

However it came about, I relished the special presents set aside until late afternoon, long after my siblings had broken or lost interest in their Christmas toys, to be opened by only me while the others sang and watched me cut my birthday cake. Tommy once referred to it as the "crappy part of Christmas day."

Midnight Mass was the calm before the storm. Captivated by the life-sized figures of Jesus, Mary, Joseph, and the shepherds in the stable, we knelt and reflected momentarily on how people celebrated Christmas in so many countries around the world. Incense and Latin assailed us, and serenity enveloped us. Leaving church, we were surprised by the scene that greeted us. "It's snowing," said Mom quietly. And it was.

Later, hopelessly trying to sleep, I lay on my stomach in the top bunk, my chin resting on my hands. Having parted the drapes, I squinted into the white swirl to see if I could spot Santa's sleigh. Publicly, in the company of my peers, I vigorously denied that Santa existed; privately, there was no theological debate battering my brain. "C'mon, old fellow. Don't let the snow slow you down. You can do it, big guy." Below me in the lower bunk, Tommy the atheist snored loudly.

We were the first ones out of bed, a carbon copy of every family in America. The sliding door to the living room barred our view; the unimaginable stood on the other side. In our parents' bedroom, their bodies lay like logs. The horribly irrational speculation that they might have died in the middle of the night occurred to us. Else why did they slumber so? It was already past five.

After flushing the toilet ten times in succession failed to rouse them, we turned to more certain methods.

"Go pinch Linda!" I ordered.

Tommy scurried off to do the deed.

A minute later, her crying awoke the folks.

"She must have had a nightmare," I volunteered.

My father glowered at me through half-closed eyelids. "I'll give you a nightmare."

"Merry Christmas, boys," said Mom, holding our still-sobbing sister. "Oh, and happy birthday, Michael."

Tommy made a face.

Dad, sitting on the edge of the bed in his boxers, his salt-and-pepper chest hairs a sharp contrast to his bare head, looked at us and grumbled. "Well, as long as we're awake, we might as well go see if you-know-who came."

If? There it was. The last minute tease. The indecisive, not-quite-sure, maybe-Rudolph-took-a-wrong-turn-and-plunged-the-sleigh-into-a-molten-volcano kind of statement that caused kids to almost wet themselves.

"I'm sure he did," reassured my mom. But the seed of nagging doubt had already been planted.

So it was with trepidation that we stormed through the door and into the living room to feast our blood-shot eyes—now filled with wonder and relief—upon the dazzling array of gifts laid out neatly by St. Nick himself.

And there it sat. Over in the corner, covering an expanse of carpet. The present that would offset the oranges and apples stuffed into our stockings; the one that would nullify the shirts and slacks hidden in neat boxes camouflaged with wrapping and ribbon. It was, without question, the grandest gift I had ever or would ever receive. I dove to the rug and reached out my hand, clutching the nearest piece. It was Abraham Lincoln, sixteenth President of the United States and Commander-in-Chief of the Union Army. Christmas had come.

CHAPTER 13

"WINTER WONDERLAND"

Meteorological records from my childhood show heavier-than-normal amounts of snowfall for the Chicago area. So, it isn't just an over-active imagination that, looking back across time, causes me to see white when envisioning winter. Those months meant snow chains for cars, snow boots for kids. Snowmen and snow forts. Skating and sledding. And, most deliciously, stalking girls we liked with snowballs. An important ritual was to carve the girl's initials into the smooth sphere—C. B. or V. F., for example—before blasting her in the back as she walked home from school. This was a fifth grade boy's way of telling a girl she was worthy of his attention.

Another target for snowballs was, of course, passing cars. Hunched for hours, hidden in clumps of evergreens, we waited for an unsuspecting motorist to drive slowly down our street. Rising like Indians from buffalo grass, we pelted the vehicle's windows, sides, and trunk, then ducked out of sight, shielded by the bushes. It never failed. Well, to be honest, there was this one time . . .

Jimmy and I were shocked once when a driver slammed on his brakes and emerged from a black Cadillac, fists clenched in rage. Immediately, he began running toward our place of concealment. Before I could even flinch, Jimmy took off, dashing madly across the snow-covered yard. I watched in disbelief as he catapulted himself over the low fence, regained his balance, and continued fleeing. I still hadn't moved a muscle, a sitting duck for the angry stranger. Grabbing my collar with one oversized, gloved hand, he lifted me off the ground. His sunken eyes fixed me with a cold stare; his breath reeked of cheap cigar. Shaking me like a dust rag, he shouted in my face, "So, you thought you'd get away, did you?"

"No, sir," I stammered. Actually, I had never considered that some grown man would waste his valuable time chasing after a couple of dopey kids who threw snowballs at cars. And if I had considered it, I would have instinctively known that Jimmy, with his track-and-field speed, would have easily escaped, leaving me behind to be beaten to a pulp by Mr. Homicidal Maniac. As I visualized my life's blood splattering onto the snow, the man dropped me unceremoniously to the ground.

"What's the matter with you? Don't you realize somebody could get hurt? You better not let me catch you throwing snowballs at cars again, you hear me? 'Cause next time I'm taking you to the police station. Do you know what they'll do to you there? They'll put you in a moldy cell and let you rot until you're old. And you'll never see your parents again either."

I was near tears.

He started to turn back to his car. "Oh, and tell your stupid friend what I said goes for him too." And then, with a final sigh of exasperation, he stalked off, his wing tips leaving giant footprints in the snow.

Later, when Jimmy finally returned, I convinced him that Mafia man meant business, and we went back to chucking at girls.

Snowball wars also engaged us. We used up many a Saturday afternoon laboriously crafting elaborate snow forts and stockpiling ammunition for an Armageddon showdown at dusk. Missiles rocketed back and forth through the still air, occasionally finding their mark. Everyone was on his honor not to cheat. If a snowball struck you in a mortal spot—head, heart, groin—you were dead, no arguments. On the other hand, a superficial wound to the arm or leg would not remove you from the battle, but you did have to throw with your unnatural arm or limp or crawl or whatever depending on where you took the "bullet." We stopped using ice balls when Jimmy took one to the eye and almost lost his sight. The doctor made him wear an eye patch to school for a month. Everyone called him Blackbeard.

On Sunday afternoons, my father gathered the family for a short drive to the forest preserve and its incredible sledding hill. Here were six or seven man-made "runs," the middle ones being the bumpiest due to overuse. Hard-packed ice, shimmering in the sun, awaited the brave soul who risked his life catapulting down it on a "flying saucer." Spinning, bouncing, gripping the rope handles, the daredevil hung on breathlessly until the circular sled plowed into the open-field runway and came to a halt, snow spraying upward into his face. Nursing a bruised bottom, the rider got off the sled, stepped quickly aside to avoid the next hurtling comet, and trudged with unwavering determination back up to the top for another go at it.

My dad's favorite winter sport was to load the entire family of five onto our toboggan and steer us down one of the smooth outer "runs," cutting precariously close to really big trees at breakneck speed. His theory must have been that an unfortunate accident would take all of us to Heaven at the same time. This never happened. But Tommy almost bought the farm one crisp, cold day in January.

The most difficult—and dangerous—aspect of the five-man toboggan was the amount of time it took to unload everyone at the bottom of the hill. Hence, the chance of someone being "picked off" by the next sled was a real threat. My dad, surprisingly swift for a big man, would always jump out, snatch up Linda with one hand, and pull my mom up by her arm. The implication of such chivalry was that we boys were supposed to be alert enough to get ourselves out of harm's way.

Swoosh.

"Get out! Move it! Everybody to the left!" shouted the commandant. The left, a wide expanse of forest, meant safety and security. I followed rapidly, my wind-stung eyes searching for a foxhole to dive into if necessary. Tommy moved to his other left.

Time stood still, a Currier and Ives landscape.

My mother screamed a belated warning.

A fiery red toboggan, another family of five aboard, lined my brother up in its sights. Trapped like a deer in the headlights, Tommy assumed a John Wayne stance as if to say: "Go on, hit me, you sons-of-bitches! I'll take one for my country!"

The blast launched his little body skyward where, like a trained acrobat, he somersaulted in space and landed hard on his back, his snowsuit barely cushioning the blow. He did not move.

Handing Linda to my mom, my father sprinted to the fallen figure.

I followed. Assuming the worst, I wondered what life would be like without him. For most of my time on earth, he had been there, annoying me. Would I miss him? Would inheriting his comic book collection compensate for the tragic loss?

My father knelt in the snow beside him. "Son, are you all right?"

"Owww," Tommy moaned.

A man approached, the driver of the hit-and-run sled. "Is he okay? I'm so sorry. He just stepped right out in front of us. I didn't have time to steer around him."

"He'll be fine," my dad answered. But his voice betrayed his lingering doubt. "Can you get up, son?"

By now, a curious crowd circled the scene.

"What hurts?"

"My legs."

Dad tugged Tommy's snow pants out of his boots and rolled them up. Ugly red welts stood out on his shins where the curved wooden bow of the sled had caught him full force.

"Will he need x-rays?" It was my mom's voice, cutting into the tension of the moment.

"Probably." Dad poked at the lumps. "Does this hurt?"

"A little," said Tommy bravely.

Suddenly, a vision came to me. It was one of Tommy-the-stout-hearted, legs in casts, ordering me around for months while he sat, feet propped on pillows, watching TV.

"Mike, get me some more ice cream, will you? And put some chocolate sauce on it while you're at it."

Leaning in, I caught his eye. His mouth twisted into a goofy grin. Was he milking this?

"Get up," I said.

Stunned spectators stared incredulously at me.

"What?" asked my father.

"I think he's okay. I've seen him in much worse shape." It was true. I had personally witnessed Tommy survive flipping over the front end of his bike on a dirt hill, falling head first off the top of a slide, and roller skating into a wooden fence post. He, like most boys, was tough, rugged, durable.

"Can you stand up?" asked Dad, a trembling hesitancy in his voice.

"I think so." And then, Lazarus-like, he rose. Gingerly, he took two steps. He did not collapse.

The people applauded in relief. Mom wept grateful tears.

Tommy spoke. "Can we go home now?"

On the way up the hill, my father pulled me aside. "How did you know he wasn't hurt bad?"

"Just a guess," I answered truthfully. Perhaps it was that. Or perhaps it was fear that he wasn't, for once, "faking it" for attention. Fear that, lying helpless in the snow, he really had broken a leg or two. I did what I had always done and bossed him to his feet. After all, that's what big brothers are for.

My black rubber boots crunched down the middle of the street. I was on my way to Bobby's house one block over. As I passed under the street lamp, it cast an eerie glow on the mounds of crusted snow piled up like canyon walls on either side. With each breath, a puff of white smoke shot out into the crystal clear night air. All around me it was silent, save for the sound of my steps. No noise emitted from the houses, sealed like tombs against the wintry frost. No cars crossed my path. It was just me and the bright stars above.

I carried in my arms, somewhat awkwardly, a game which entertained Bobby and me on winter nights such as this one. It was an official NHL Hockey game, only a year old and already beaten up around the edges. Rectangular in shape, it was a rink with lines and circles, goals and players. The latter were made of metal, and—unlike later versions—featured interchangeable teams.

In fact, all six NHL teams were included, each set of men encased in small paper sacks. The Canadians, Maple Leafs, and Bruins wore dark home colors; the Black Hawks, Red Wings, and Rangers were decked out in visitors' white. The pucks were made of wood—again, later versions reduced the puck to plastic.

This was the second year in which Bobby and I had battled each other, and we had both become, through hours of fun, quite skilled. This year, we decided to imitate the Stanley Cup playoffs, choosing four teams and working our way through the seven game semi-finals and championship round. Tonight: semi-final, game four; second place Black Hawks (me) versus fourth place Maple Leafs (Bobby). The Leafs led the series two games to one, so I was particularly focused as I approached Bobby's driveway.

Unable to ring the bell without setting the game down, I nudged the storm door open using my shoulder and elbow, then kicked the big door hard three times.

Bobby's sister Cyndi, one year younger, opened the door. "Hi. C'mon in. Bobby, Mike's here!"

Stepping in, I looked at her. Simply put, she was luscious. Black hair in bangs, brown eyes, pretty smile, the works. Years later, I would fall heavily for her—one in a series of unrequited loves that would mark my adolescent years. For now, I could only return her smile, the warmth of the room causing liquid snot to run out of my nose into the corners of my mouth.

Bobby saved the day by bounding down the stairs yelling, "And the Leafs take a commanding three to one series lead by shutting out the mighty Hawks!"

Setting down the game and wiping the sleeve of my coat across my dripping nose, I retorted, "Not if Bobby Hull has anything to say about it!"

Bobby Hull. The Golden Jet. Weeks earlier, my dad had taken me to my first professional hockey game at the old Chicago Stadium. First balcony seats. Cigar smoke from below drifting up into our faces. The Black Hawks wearing their home jerseys—a vibrant red. Having seen them only on WGN-TV, wearing their road white jerseys—and on a black and white set no less—I was astounded. But the most amazing thing, without a doubt, was how the ancient palace was transformed whenever Bobby Hull picked up the puck behind the net and charged up ice. Electricity crackled as a delirious roar of anticipation almost raised the roof. Spectators, arms in the air, rose as one to cheer their hero. Since that night—when Hull led the Hawks to victory with a "hat trick," and crazed fans flung their fedoras onto the ice—I had spoken of little else, which clearly annoyed Bobby.

"Bobby, schmobby. You forget that Johnny Bower will be in goal to block all of Hull's shots. Just like the last game." This barb was a stinging reminder of last night's game, when the Maple Leafs' goalie had swept aside the last five Hull slap shots in an eventual one-point victory.

"Not tonight!"

And so it went. Two friends locked in a fierce duel as an antidote for the harshness of bitter winter nights. At times, the board leapt off the dining room table as one of us pushed a player forward, and the puck "clanged" into the metal net. "A shot and a goal!" followed, a tribute to the legendary Lloyd Pettit, greatest of all hockey announcers.

The game, like real life, moved fast, and mistakes—a missed open shot or a goalie out of position—had consequences, albeit minor ones. So, we played with passion, wrists constantly in motion, twisting-turning-pulling-punching the long, silver rods. We were the hockey gods, whose deft movements controlled the fate of a team, a city, a nation.

This warfare had everything: exultation and damnation; "the thrill of victory and the agony of defeat." Regardless of the outcome, however, we bonded in the spirit of friendship, and this would keep us content for many a season to come.

"See ya tomorrow night!" yelled Bobby at my back, which was now halfway down the driveway. The door slammed behind me—a little too hard, I thought.

"And we're even," I said to the silent street ahead of me. My boots crunched homeward.

CHAPTER 14

"TV TIME (BUCKETS OF FUN)"

"Hey, kids, what time is it?" Any self-respecting boy or girl from this era knew, of course, the answer. Our generation was the first to be weaned on television. From the very hour of our births, TV kicked off what came to be known in later years as its "Golden Age." It featured Lucy and Ethel wrapping chocolates, Ralph and Norton scheming to get rich, Matt Dillon blasting away at the bad guys, and Flash Gordon saving earth from Ming the Merciless and his terrifying death ray. During lunch hour, we wolfed down grilled cheese sandwiches with Campbell's Tomato Soup while watching Bozo. After school, we were entertained by Annette—performing with the lesser Mouseketeers—and never missed an episode of the "Hardy Boys" or "Spin and Marty." The very fabric of our core values was woven from Superman's creed: "Truth, Justice, and the American Way." And the Lone Ranger's never-ending fight for right gave us a larger-than-life hero to embrace.

Tommy and I loved the Lone Ranger above all the other TV gods. And why not? Ambushed by outlaws, gunned down with other Texas Rangers, rescued by Tonto, the mask cut from his dead brother's vest, he embodied the solitary Western hero. The fact that his faithful sidekick was an Indian made him especially undesirable to innocent, law-abiding townsfolk, who were always surprised by his sudden appearance wherever there was trouble. But in the end, wary or not, they accepted him as he cleaned up the mess and moved on to the next town. "Say, who was that masked man, anyway?"

My brother and I spent many a day emulating the heroics of the pair. Tommy was Tonto, a role for which I deemed him particularly well suited. He ran around in a cheap buckskin jacket with a headband and feather saying things like: "Mmm, Kemosabe, me think gang try to rob stagecoach again today." Resplendent in white hat, black mask, and gun belt with silver bullets, I'd respond in a condescending tone, "For once you might be right, Tonto. We'd better ride ahead and cut them off at the pass." We'd gallop off to spend the rest of the day chasing invisible bad guys from room to room around the house.

Our Lone Ranger fetish went so far as to make us want to eat Cheerios every day of the week. Not anywhere near as tasty as the many sugared cereals on the market, they were nonetheless the show's sponsor and thus worthy of our consumption. But there was further incentive to have our mom purchase the product. On the backs of the boxes, there was an assortment of cardboard cutouts that, in their entirety, made up an authentic Western town. The buildings included: a general store, a livery stable, a post office, a hotel, a saloon, and a jail. All one had to do was keep eating enough of the crap and, with each empty box, take a scissors and— voila—another piece of the puzzle. The problem was "doubles." No real Western town had two jails and no livery stable, or vice versa. So, whenever Mom headed off to the grocery store, we pleaded with her to make sure she bought only the boxes with the buildings we needed.

"Remember, Mom, no more general stores! We've already got two! We need the saloon or the hotel. Please look for them, okay?"

She would leave and return all smiles, and we would tear apart the paper bags to find the bright yellow boxes. And there, staring out at us would be . . .

"A general store? Mom! What about the saloon? Or the hotel? Those were the ones we needed!"

"Well, I looked. I couldn't find them. There were some boxes on the top shelf, but I couldn't reach that high. When you finish this box, I'll buy some more. Until then, you'll just have to be patient."

Patience was one thing. Gagging down a completely useless box of unsweetened cereal was quite another. However, it really didn't matter because, until we saved up some money, our town with three general stores and no saloon or hotel was nothing but a "ghost" town, desolate clumps of tumbleweed rolling through in the wind. It needed men, and we had none. Yet. This was the "catch" to the giveaway on the box. For a sum of $1.85 plus shipping and handling, we could own a set of rubber figures much like my Civil War set. These included: The Lone Ranger and his horse Silver, Tonto—who had no horse and so apparently had to walk alongside of the masked man—and the evil Butch Cavendish with a handful of his gang. The slight to Tonto notwithstanding, this was an awesome collection of men and a "must have" for any Lone Ranger fan.

So, we volunteered to do some extra chores around the house, saved some money, and finally sent away for the set. We had since acquired a hotel but were still missing the saloon. I understood why one day when I overheard my mom remark to my dad, "They don't need a saloon. It's a bad influence on them." What would she have said—or done—if there was a brothel in the town?

The day the set arrived by mail in a shoebox-sized container, Tommy and I let out a war whoop and raced to open it. There were Butch and his boys, back in black; there was Tonto in red—could they have been more overtly racist?—and the Lone Ranger in light blue. His legs were spread apart in an obscene fashion so he could mount Silver. But where the blazes was Silver?

"Mom! Silver's not here!"

Bustling into the living room, she grabbed the box and shook it vigorously upside down. Thin sheets of tissue paper drifted slowly to the floor. It was true. Silver, the Lone Ranger's beautiful white stallion, was missing.

"Don't worry," comforted my mom. "We'll write to the company. It'll only take a few weeks."

Oh, great, I thought. And until then the Lone Ranger could waddle around with a bad case of saddle rash.

By the time Silver arrived—months, not weeks, later—the cheap cardboard buildings could barely stand on their own, we still didn't have a saloon thanks to our Carrie Nation-like mom, and Tommy had flushed Tonto down the toilet in a fit of rage at being typecast as my "faithful Indian companion." And so our quest to own the perfect Western town and populate it with heroes and villains rode off into the sunset like the Lone Ranger himself. "Hi-yo, Silver, away!"

"Who's your favorite clown?" Perched over our TV trays, we heard the answer shouted out by the grandparents, parents, and lucky kids who had gotten tickets to "Bozo's Circus." The show was then in its infancy, before it became the hottest ticket in town with a wait of up to ten years, and our dream was to someday sit in the stands and take in the fun and games.

"Bozo, the World's Greatest Clown!" continued Ned Locke. "With Oliver O. Oliver, Sandy the Tramp, Ringmaster Ned—that's me—Bob Trendler and his Big Top Band, and a cast of thousands!"

"No way there's a thousand people there," said Tommy, a string of grilled cheese hanging from his chin.

"How do you know?" In fact, everyone knew. But I challenged him mostly to annoy.

"Well, maybe . . ." he hesitated, backing down.

Mom entered the room and turned down the volume on the TV.

"Hey . . ." I started.

"Guess what? I have a surprise for you. Grandpa just called; a friend gave him four tickets to Bozo for next week. We'll leave Linda with Grandma and all go."

She might as well have said, "The Cubs won the pennant!" We spent the next five minutes jumping up and down and turning somersaults on the carpet. Oh, happy day!

Our teachers were equally enthusiastic. Mr. Paducci told the class of my good fortune, adding that it was a "special event" and therefore a valid reason to miss school. Yeah, I thought, unlike Dale the Bully, who missed a day every other week to hang out at the train station and practice his skills as a novice pickpocket.

When Grandpa picked us up in his maroon Oldsmobile on that snowy Tuesday in late January, we had been given barber shop haircuts and wore our nicest shirts, slacks, and dress shoes. Mom wasn't going to have her children embarrass the family on TV. Avoiding the newfangled expressway, it took Grandpa a good hour and a half in the blinding snow to get to the WGN station where the show was filmed, but we made it in plenty of time.

Ushered onto the set after standing in line for half an hour, we met the show's assistant producer. Tommy immediately dubbed him "Son of Hitler." He yelled at us as he arranged us in the grandstand, instructing us how to behave and rehearsing us with giant cue cards. When the show began, I was amazed by two things: first was how Ringmaster Ned had his back to us almost the entire time as he talked into the camera; second was how close the cameras were to the clown action, making me wonder why we couldn't see them on TV.

Bozo (Bob Bell) and Oliver O. Oliver (Ray Rayner) matched wits in the first sketch, which ended with the latter getting a pie in the face, hysterical stuff for kids who had been brought up on the Three Stooges. Then, during a commercial break, I was stunned when Tommy was chosen to play in a game. Sibling jealously reared its ugly head. This bites, I thought. My little brother gets to go out onto the floor and run around while I just sit here watching him. What kind of benevolent God would allow this to happen?

To make matters worse, his team won the carry-the-Styrofoam-ball-on-the-spoon relay race. But, of course, equal opportunity Bozo had stupid prizes for everyone: dolls for the loser girls and sleek racing cars for the geeky boys. Tommy, grinning, climbed back up to our seats, where I ignored him.

From this point on, my only hope for salvation was to be chosen to play the granddaddy of all TV games, the Bozo Buckets. Long before the Bozo-puter chose a boy and a girl in a fair, random manner, one's fate was determined by the truly wacky, "who-the-hell-ever-thought-this-one-up?" magic arrows. To select the players, the camera flitted crazily back and forth across the screen, abruptly jerking to a halt and zooming in on a pack of wild mongrel children, each of whom would stick a shiv in his closest friend for a shot at immortality on the "Grand Prize Game." Invariably, the biggest kid, often a pre-teen with a ducktail and zits, shoved the younger children away and stuck his fat face into the center of the lens right between the blinking arrows. Bozo, hyperventilating, shouted out, "We've got our boy!" and the lunk-head lumbered down to play, usually cleaning up in the process. Well, by God, I was the big kid now, eleven years old, and nobody was going to keep me from every Chicago kid's dream.

After more clown skits and an acrobatic performance, it was finally time. The camera lurched to the right, away from where we were seated. The eager, hungry faces mooned upward. It stopped on the first row. A set-up. Some rich snot had been hand picked before the show. I had been screwed over.

"It's a girl!" yelled Bozo.

"Now, let's find a boy!" cried Ringmaster Ned.

The tension spider-webbed down our backs into our arms and legs. Teeth were clenched; fists were balled.

The cameraman was caught up in the frenzy of it all. Back and forth. Up and down. Back and forth. Stop! Stop! Stop! When it froze, it was as far away from me as wrong is from right. Slumping, I buried my aching head in my hands.

"AAAAAAAAARGH!" Was Bozo vomiting or what? "It's another girl!" he wailed. "We have to find a boy!"

Reprieve. The camera spun in spasmodic circles like an abandoned spaceship hurtling through the galaxy. It came close, closer, closest. Zoom now! The earth stood still. My saucer-like eyes reflected off the camera's motionless, giant eyeball. Resurrection.

"It's a boy!" a distant voice echoed from far away. My mom grabbed my arm, hauled me to my feet, and turned me to face her. She wetted her fingers and slicked down my cowlick. "Your zipper's not open, is it?" she whispered.

I checked; it was closed. "Go," she said, guiding me gently through the crowd. Slowly, I stepped on the risers, moving ever closer to fame and fortune. I could almost taste its sweet nectar.

"And what's your name?" asked Bozo.

"Rebecca," answered the girl in the plaid skirt and saddle shoes.

"And how about you, young fellow?" Bozo leaned closer to me.

"Mike," I squeaked out. Damn, that clown was big.

"Well, Mike, why don't you take this silver dollar and walk over and drop it in Bucket #6?"

In the early days of Bozo, before the producers settled on a consistent, flat fee of fifty dollars, Bucket #6 was loaded one dollar at a time in an ever-increasing amount until someone hit the jackpot. The worst-case scenario was for a kid to hit it a day or two after someone else had done it. "Whoa! He did it! He wins two silver dollars!"

I did as I was told. The coin clinked onto the top of what looked like a sizable heap of change. It was. "Whoa! That makes sixty-four silver dollars in Bucket #6!"

Little Rebecca, whom I judged to be in about first grade, went three buckets and out. I was next. Mr. Ned was responsible for lining up the shooter. If the child's toes were over the line by a quarter of an inch, old Ned would look down upon him as if he were one of Fagin's kids and say, "You're fudging."

Nobody in the history of the show ever missed Bucket #1. Toddlers in diapers stood staring up at the spectre of a macabre clown while Mr. Ned shook the frightened child's arm until he dropped the ping-pong ball into the pail. I took a deep breath, leaned forward, extended my arm downward, and let go.

"Whoa!" shouted Bozo as if he'd just won the trifecta at Arlington Park.

I won McDonald's coupons and a free hairdo for my mom.

Bucket #2. Another cinch. I won some ice cream bars and stockings for my mom. Great. So far Mom was doing better than I was, and she wasn't even playing.

That's okay. Bucket #3 was when all the real toys started coming. Little Rebecca had claimed one sweet doll for herself when she'd hit this bucket. Just stay cool.

Sweat was dripping from my hair and into my eyes. The TV lights were incredibly hot, and Bozo was hovering again. Back off, clown, or I'll take you down. I wiped my forehead. I knew what Bozo was up to. His trick was to distract kids or make them nervous so they'd miss. His most infamous ploy was to keep the ball out of the anxious hands of a red-hot shooter who'd quickly rung up the first five. He'd pace up and down in his size 24 wides saying, "Bucket #6. Shhh. Be quiet. If he makes this, he'll win a trazillion silver dollars, a new bike, and the keys to a mansion in Beverly Hills. (Long pause) Drum roll, please." By the time the kid touched the ball again, his eyes were misty, his legs were jelly, and his pants were wet. He had a snowball's chance in Hell to win, usually missing the final bucket by forty-five feet.

But old Bozo wasn't gonna psyche me out. I nailed Bucket #3. Finally, a board game. Oliver O. Oliver held it up to the crowd as if it were a bag of gold. What? Chutes and Ladders? Why, that was for little kids. Even my baby sister had outgrown that, preferring to eat the cardboard people. Why not stick me with Candy Land? At this point, I was painfully aware that I had yet to win anything as good as the car Tommy had gotten for his pathetic spoon race.

Okay, this was it. The beginning of some major hardware with Bucket #4. Concentrate. Easy does it. A nice, soft, underhand pitch.

But in the end, I tied with the first grade girl, three buckets apiece. I spent the rest of my youth defending the missed free throw with some of the most outrageous excuses ever invented by a tormented child. The bright lights blinded me; Ringmaster Ned hurried me; Bozo flashed me. It didn't matter. No one believed me. They knew as well as I that I had simply choked. I was now prepared to spend my life identifying with Chicago's sports teams.

My mom was gracious, praising my effort while clinging to her freebies. My grandfather consoled me with some story from his youth that involved betting on a lame horse and losing the family's milk money. Tommy, clutching his car, giggled all the way home.

The next day, home for lunch, we watched a fourth grade girl run the table, netting sixty-five silver dollars. Just think, had Bozo not gotten inside my head, she would have been only a dollar richer.

CHAPTER 15

"LIGHTS OUT!"

February was an awesome month for us school children. Not only was it a mere twenty-eight days long, but we got off Lincoln's birthday (the twelfth), Washington's birthday (the twenty-second), and celebrated Valentine's Day (the fourteenth) with a big in-school party. Even in fifth grade—our last year of elementary school before the big move to junior high—we were forced to be creative with old shoeboxes: wrap in red paper, paste lacy hearts or cupids on the sides, cut a slit on the top, print our names neatly in black crayon, and there it was. When our artwork was finished a week early, Mr. Paducci announced to the class, "Now, we'll place them along the window-ledge side by side, and when you arrive at school in the mornings, just walk over and put your valentines in the boxes."

This was perfect. I could spend all of Abe's birthday creating a special, homemade valentine for Mary Linder. Maybe I could even write a poem for her:

Mary, I love you,
It's a love that's true,
So don't make me blue,
Say you love me too.

Then again . . .

"Remember," warned Mr. Paducci, "no playing favorites. You must give a valentine to every person in the class. And I'll be checking the boxes every day, so make sure that you do. We'll open them on Valentine's Day."

Every person? What horseshit was this? Did that mean I had to give one to Sandy Alstrom, who smelled funny because her little sister peed on everything in her house? Or Barbara Zeitler, who had been stuck up ever since she had been chosen to play the Snow Queen in the second grade play? Or worse, Dale the Bully, who might take offense at receiving a cute little cupid saying "Be Mine"?

This policy was astronomically unfair. If Mary got valentines from every creep in the room, how would she know it was I who really loved her? True, she had not balked at the chalk message on the playground, and yes, she suspected I was the ringleader of the infamous Jack-O-Splosion on Halloween night, but a personalized "I love you more than anyone in the whole wide world" valentine without any sleazy competition would seal the deal for me. If only . . .

I spent the twelfth signing my name to all the small, insipid Walgreens' valentines with messages like "You're My Sweetie Pie" and "Hi, Baby Cakes." Then, I took out the large one I had purchased, set it on the table, and looked lovingly at it. There was a globe spinning around on the front with the words "Love Makes the World Go 'Round." On the inside was the racy "You Make MY World Go 'Round." Hiding it from my mom, I quickly signed it, sealed it, and wrote Mary's name on the envelope. Of course, I didn't sign my own name to it. Instead, the mysterious, daring "You Know Who ? ? ?" appeared in its place. Half my battle plan was complete.

Two days later, I made sure I left early for school. Arriving first to my empty classroom, I hurriedly shoved valentines into each box, saving Mary's for last. Grabbing her shoebox with both hands, I sprinted to the wastebasket and shook the contents out. Next, I opened it and crammed my extra-large offering inside. Sure, it was a stupid-crazy act of desperation, but cupid's arrow had wounded my heart. How else could I behave? I set the box back in the nick of time.

"Hello, Mike." Mr. Paducci's voice came from the doorway. "You're here awfully early this morning, aren't you?"

"Uh, yeah," I mumbled nervously. "I'm excited about the party."

Later, the room moms delivered candy, cupcakes, and ice cream. Before the festivities began, Mr. Paducci got our attention. "Boys and girls, before we open our boxes, there is something I'd like to show you. Mary, would you bring your Valentine's box up here?"

I froze.

The class looked curiously at Mary.

She cautiously approached Mr. Paducci's desk. Taking the box from her, he removed the top, turned it upside down, and shook it. Nothing fell out.

"You see," he said. "It's empty. Some very naughty person has tried to ruin Mary's Valentine's Day. Shame on that person." Then, in another dramatic gesture, he reached down, picked up the wastebasket, raised it aloft, and dumped its contents on his desk. The class gasped.

"Here, Mary," he said in a kind voice, "are your valentines."

She scooped them up and walked self-consciously back to her seat, sympathetic eyes cast upon her.

Mr. Paducci looked sternly over the class. "If I ever find out who threw Mary's valentines away, I will mete out a severe punishment."

God forgive me. My twisted scheme had backfired. I was caught in my own sordid web of deceit. From a million miles away, Mr. Paducci's voice rang out. "Now, class, you may look at your valentines."

Later that afternoon, I slumped dejectedly over the drinking fountain, trying to drown my well-deserved sorrows. Not even Mary's sweet "Cutie Pie" valentine to me could ease my heartache. Unexpectedly, there she was, gliding past me, an angel in a red and white cotton dress. Did she suspect? Had she come to redeem me? "I noticed," she stated sarcastically, "that you couldn't be bothered to send me a valentine. Thanks. Thanks a bunch."

I slurped down another half gallon of water and headed home, mulling love's cruel ironies. I came to the conclusion that Mr. Paducci knew all along that I was the culprit. Perhaps he had observed me from the doorway that morning as I committed the crime. Thus, the removal of my valentine to Mary, the setup, and the payback. Ashamed of my act, I drifted away from Mary after that dark day. It was just as well. In my desire to attract her attention, I had sacrificed my integrity, and all the valentines in the world couldn't buy it back. As I shuffled home, head down in disgrace, I reached into my pocket for a pink, heart-shaped piece of candy to assuage my pain. I glanced at it before popping it into my mouth. It read: "Love's Fool."

Washington's birthday fell on a Friday in my fifth grade year—a much-anticipated three-day weekend, especially following the valentine fiasco. Typical for near the end of February, the deep piles of winter's snow were receding, and warmer weather was predicted. The possibilities were endless. Little did we suspect that Mother Nature had other plans.

Thursday afternoon, we trudged home on slushy sidewalks coated with wet, heavy snow mixed with falling rain from above. By evening, raindrops slid to the ends of eaves and branches, hung in suspending motion, and fell heavily to the earth. By nightfall, the temperature plunged, the dripping ceased, and the neighborhood fell silent. The street lamp shone on the crystalline branches, bending downward under the weight of their icy coats. The streets and sidewalks reflected the light like mirrors. Massive telephone and electrical poles, encased in glass, stood like sentries keeping watch over the frozen landscape. The iceman had cometh.

Halfway through "Zorro," the power went out. Sudden heavy winds had seen to that, splitting a thick, wooden electrical pole in half as if it was a toothpick.

"Oh, man!" I wailed. "Just when Zorro was sneaking up behind fat old Sergeant Garcia."

"Don't call anyone fat," reprimanded my mother, her voice sounding even more authoritarian in the dark. "Let's light some candles."

And so my family was transported back to the first century. No lights, no record players, no TV. We might as well have been cast into an ancient Roman prison with stone walls and straw on the floor. If we'd been hung in chains, we couldn't have been unhappier.

"What're we supposed to do now?" complained Tommy.

"I know," said Mom cheerfully. "As soon as I get Linda tucked in bed, the rest of us can play a game together. It will be a night of family fun."

Whoopee, I thought, but didn't dare to say out loud when my father quickly echoed Mom's sentiment. Good old "Family Fun." Translation: Monopoly by candle-light.

For that's what it was. There really wasn't an option. The granddaddy of games, it was all one needed in order to learn the peaks and valleys of American capitalism. One individual, hoarding Boardwalk, Park Place, and the four railroads, with a string of hotels up and down the boulevards, brought everybody else, with much weeping and gnashing of teeth, to their knees. Our game board gave visual testimony to that. In the middle were the jagged scars that had been inflicted upon it one night when, having been wiped out by me, Tommy snatched a butcher knife from the counter and lashed out. Foaming at the mouth, he shouted over and over with each downward stroke, "I hate this game!" He was finally subdued when Dad was able to wrestle the weapon from his pudgy little fingers.

Truth be told, everyone hated this game—if you lost. To lose in Monopoly was to be buried alive in methodical fashion. The final roll of the dice, like the last shovelful of dirt, sealed your fate. You moved your marker slowly, space by space, looking hesitantly up at your competitors to see if anyone would throw you a life preserver, and then pushed across the table all your worldly paper possessions—money, deeds, even the stupid "Get Out of Jail Free" card that you had hung onto for the past three and a half hours. The others cast their judgmental eyes upon you as if to say, "Loser," which you most certainly were.

To win, however, was to experience the gambler's euphoria—another evil lesson for children to learn. You had risked some multi-colored cash to put up those houses a while back, and the profits were rightfully gained. There was nothing like the dizzy sensation of vain pride that came with achieving happiness at the expense of someone else's misery. You were rich, like the gentleman with the top hat and tuxedo, and the poor would just have to fend for themselves.

The game, like all popular board games, began innocently enough—the kitchen knives had been locked in the cupboard. Players chose the silver pieces. I always picked the race car; Tommy, the dog. After that, avarice was to the forefront. Strategy had surprisingly little to do with the outcome, although Tommy always tried to collect all the railroads so he could wear us down bit by bit with each trip around the board. My father made me quit and go to bed one night when, angry at having landed on a railroad for the umpteenth time, I scowled at Tommy as I threw the money across the table at him and said, "You sure love your damn railroads, don't you, Nancy-boy?"

If the object of the game was to create an ambiance of fun and fellowship, Monopoly failed miserably. By the end of that candle-lit evening, I was pouting because no one ever landed on my Park Place/Boardwalk hotels, and I eventually had to sell them off during my downward spiral. Meanwhile, Tommy was in tears and threatening to burn down the house with the candles, Dad was screaming at him, and Mom—the "winner"—was left alone at the kitchen table to put away the game. Congratulations, Mom! We went to bed that night exhausted, crabby, and hoping the power would be restored while we slept. We were in for a long wait.

The next morning, ice world greeted us. Dad had left for work, and Mom had removed perishables such as milk, eggs, and butter to the back stoop to keep them cold. Blinking, I stared incredulously out the kitchen window to see Bobby and Jimmy playing ice hockey in the middle of the street. Excited to join them, we donned our skates and went out the door into the freezing air.

"Here we come!" I shouted as we skated atop the glazed sidewalk. We sped down the driveway and out onto our own private rink.

For the next two hours, joined by Johnny, Eddie, Denny, and Greg, we abandoned all reason, skates slicing through the icy veneer, sticks steering the frozen puck across the smooth surface, smiling and shouting with slap-happy insanity. Occasionally, a car came slip-sliding down the street toward us, and someone would warn, "Look out! Here comes the Zamboni!"

Jimmy took a puck above his left eye. "Don't worry! I'm okay!" he yelled as blood dripped off his cheek, splashing to the ice below. "Let's keep playing!"

And we did. We played until the sun came out and melted away our fun. Skates began to catch, and I found myself face down in what was rapidly becoming water. "We gotta quit," said Bobby, stating the obvious.

That was Friday at noon. The rest of the day was spent in the increasingly waning hope that the power would come back on and we could watch TV. By Friday evening, when Family Fun II—Parcheesi—had replaced "Soupy Sales" and "Rawhide," it was clear to us that we would be stranded on this particular island for some time to come.

Saturday was spent by natural light doing some homework, cleaning out closets, working on art projects at the kitchen table—Mom's idea to inspire our creativity—and finally, Family Fun III, a rousing game of Disney Dominos. Come soon, sweet Savior.

After Sunday Mass—St. Paul's, with its connections, had power to spare—Dad took us out for a restaurant meal, a rare treat. We had pancakes and waffles. The syrup cap, suspiciously loose after Tommy used it, came off and drowned my meal. When Linda reached into her water glass and threw ice cubes at the waitress, Dad said it was time to go. Tommy absconded with seventeen sugar packets in the inside pockets of his blazer.

Sunday afternoon, I sat at the old wooden desk in the corner of my bedroom and poured out my heart in a love letter to Annette Funicello. The power came back on in time to watch "Ed Sullivan" while Mom ironed our school clothes for Monday. During a commercial, Dad, perpetually wise, turned to us and said, "Well, boys, I think it was good for all of us to get a small taste of what life was like for our founding fathers. Imagine George Washington growing up as a young boy without the comforts we take for granted. TV, for instance."

"Yeah," I said unwisely, "that's probably why he took an axe and chopped down the cherry tree. Too many 'Family Fun' nights."

And an early bedtime for me.

CHAPTER 16

"UPCHUCKIN' ON THE OREGON TRAIL"

Winter melted slowly into spring. Baseball started up again, and all seemed right with the world. There was, however, an uneasy feeling that began to come over me; time was winding down on a major segment of my life. The familiar routine of elementary school was fading, and the shadow of the unknown loomed ominously on the pathway ahead. We had heard stories about the junior high we would attend, located on the other side of the tracks.

First, there was the trauma of the bus, where sixth graders were karate-chopped by the older kids as they stumbled their way through the gauntlet of the center aisle, desperately seeking an empty seat. "Can't sit here, moron!" "Keep movin', dork!" Finally, the bruised and battered child, fighting back tears, was forced to sit in the back of the bus, where pimple-faced greasers smoked cigarettes and belched their names loudly.

Next came the death march into the imposing building itself, complete with endless crisscrossing corridors, neat rows of metal lockers, and "UP" and "DOWN" staircases. The novice would move mindlessly through the sea of swarming bodies, clutching his brown paper lunch sack in one hand, his combination lock and a pair of No. 2 pencils in the other. Buried as deep as Coronado's gold in his pants pocket was his schedule, which had arrived in the mail a few days earlier. The schedule included all of his classes, most with different teachers in different rooms in different parts of the gigantic building. The teachers each had a unique reputation. Miss Meese, the sixth grade LASS teacher, was rumored to be in her mid-eighties, had never married or owned a TV, and generally hated kids, boys in particular. Mr. Watson, the math and science teacher, spoke in a monotone, gave frequent detentions, and loaded mountains of homework upon his students.

Also on the schedule were two items that made the blood run cold: lunch and gym. The former provided twenty-five minutes in the middle of the day for kids to stand in line to buy either milk to complement their brown-bag sandwiches or an entire, well-balanced hot lunch. My Catholic friends cautioned me, if I planned on buying lunch on Fridays, to get in line early. The cafeteria ladies made only so many cheese pizza bagels for the minority who couldn't eat meat, and some Protestant kids lied about their religion just to get the cheese ones—probably because the sausage was rumored to be dog food. This left nada for the persecuted Catholics at the end of the long line.

Gym class featured the horror of entering a foul, mold-covered locker room, stripping in front of others, changing into truly embarrassing shorts and T-shirts, working up a sweat for forty minutes under the tutelage of a sneering sadist, showering briefly, and changing back into school clothes, the now damp shirt sticking to one's chest and back during his next class. Once a week was coed gym, which unfortunately did not include showering with the girls.

However, boys' gym did allow an adult with unique gifts—one who would normally work as a prison guard—an opportunity to earn a living by throwing out medicine balls, paddling those who misbehaved, and laughing at the misfortunes of others. Always amusing to these caretakers of youth was the sound of rubber smacking against flesh, most prevalent in the game of bombardment, called dodge ball by some. They howled with delight whenever an unsuspecting sixth grader, huddled in the corner to avoid the onslaught of the eighth graders, caught one square in his fat thigh, causing a red mark that would gradually disappear over the next two years. "Nice shot, Billy!" came the congratulatory bark, while the crippled kid crawled to the sidelines with tears streaming down his face, wondering if he'd ever walk again.

These, and other Poe-like tales, were spewed like lava at the fifth graders as if to temper our tenure as top dogs. All too soon our reign would end, and we would be flung to the bottom of the putrid pit that was junior high. But until that dreadful day, we could continue on and at least try to enjoy our final days of childhood. That is, if nothing went wrong.

At this tempestuous age, kids disliked other kids for a variety of reasons. The playground heard comments like: "I don't like him. He has B.O." or "Don't let him play. He can't catch." But a valid reason for not wanting to be anywhere near a kid, whether in class or at recess, was if he had once and forever stigmatized himself by throwing up at school. This was a sin that could not be forgiven through penance. The concept was not a complex one: once a kid had hurled all over himself, his desk, and perhaps others, he was likely to repeat the act again at any time. He wore the mark of the beast as clearly as if it had been burned into his forehead. It read: "Stay away from me! I may be a nice guy, but I have no self-control! URRRRRP!"

By fifth grade, it was clear that I was above this. Having never thrown up at school, I was not cursed company. I could—and did—look arrogantly down on those who had gotten sick, and I judged them harshly. And then, on a sunny Monday in April, the black clouds of fate rolled in over me.

The morning began with an air-raid drill. A product of the Cold War, it was one of several antidotes for the Soviet Union's capability of annihilating the United States with nuclear weapons. Upon hearing the series of short, foghorn-like blasts, we filed out of the room and lined up in the hallway. There, pressed against the wall, we dropped to our hands and knees and tucked our heads into our chests, covering the backs of our necks with our arms. The theory—apparently logical to our govern-ment—was a simple one: if the warhead of an atomic bomb landed on someone's ass, that kid would not be seriously harmed. And this would turn out to be the gen-eration that grew up to distrust our country's leaders?

When the blaring noise ceased, we froze momentarily. Safe. A false alarm. Now nearly deaf, we rose as one. I felt a sudden wave of nausea, but this was not unusual. Blood had been rushing to my head for five minutes, and it always took me time to regain my "sea" legs.

Back in the classroom, Skeeter Dawkins expressed disappointment that it had only been a drill. He thought it would be "cool" to be bombed. The rest of us were thankful to get back to our projects in one piece. Mr. Pa-ducci had devised end-of-the-year packets designed to keep us busy, and subsequently quiet, until June. The theme was Western expansion, and we were required to complete maps, graphs, artwork, journal writing, and vocabulary definitions. I determined that I would rather have crossed the plains and mountains with the Donner Party than attempt to finish this by the end of school.

As I sat tracing with colored pencils the path of the Oregon Trail, I noticed that I still felt queasy. Perhaps a drink of water would make my stomach stop hurting. Receiving permission from Mr. Paducci, I left the room, returning moments later. I had merely taken a few sips from the drinking fountain and felt no better.

Now, as I looked down at my work, the nineteenth century U.S. map in front of me was spinning. The Sioux and Cheyenne Nations, once carefully separated by color, blended together in a whirling, kaleidoscopic maze; and steamboats placed precisely atop the mighty Mississippi slid across the Great Plains toward the Rockies. Looking up, I saw that my classmates, seated at their desks, were moving too, gliding in a square-dance-gone-sour around and around me. It finally hit me; I was going to be sick.

Had my mother not raised me to be polite, I could have made it to the toilet with time to spare. No such smarts here. I moved instead toward the front of the room and Mr. Paducci's desk to ask his permission to go to the bathroom. There, standing between us, was Gabby Gustoson. Appropriately nicknamed, that girl loved to talk. She especially loved to talk to Mr. Paducci, on whom she had a major crush. Once, in an attempt to attract his attention on the playground, she had grabbed the sleeve of his sports jacket and yanked on it until she split the seam. This time, she was leaning on his desk, giggling and flirting while asking stupid questions about wagon train travel.

"So, what did the pioneers do when they had to go to the bathroom?"

I was gone. Maybe her reference to "bathroom" had been the final impetus. It didn't matter now. What mattered was that somehow I had to make it to the end of the hall. The last thing I saw as I lunged for the classroom door was Mark Von Better's quizzical smile asking me what I was up to.

As I pushed open the door, up it came. In a feeble, last-ditch effort to stop it, I clasped my fingers over my mouth as I ran. It was like trying to stop a fast-moving train. Filling my cheeks momentarily, it burst forth, geyser-like, spraying out the sides.

Finished in the bathroom, I tiptoed through the slick mine field back to class. Incredibly, no one was yet aware of my mishap, and I toyed with the idea of sitting down and continuing my work as if nothing out of the ordinary had occurred. But as I stood sheet-white in the doorway, dribbles of puke staining my shirt, there was nowhere to hide. My peers glared with disdain in my direction. "Leper" hung silently on their lips. I approached Mr. Paducci's desk where, not surprisingly, Gabby was still engaged in one-sided conversation. I stood motionless, head lowered, until I caught their attention. Mercifully, Gabby stopped chattering in mid-sentence.

"Mike," said Mr. Paducci, "you threw up, didn't you?"
Ah, you couldn't fool old Mr. P.

I rode my bike home fifteen minutes later. Before I left, however, I endured further humiliation when the custodian came and dusted the hallway with orange-red sawdust. It stretched out forever, like the Oregon Trail. As if that wasn't bad enough, Mrs. Sutter across the hall took her fourth graders to the gym to finish their lesson because, in her words, "It smells so bad my kids can't learn."

I barfed three more times that day, proving Mr. Paducci's wisdom in sending me home. It was a full-blown stomach flu, late in the season but potent nonetheless. My mom allowed me to return to school for a half day on Friday.

I was understandably anxious to enter the classroom again, fully expecting to see my classmates in suits of armor—or at least raincoats. But they welcomed me back in magnanimous fashion, graciously assuming that lightning wouldn't strike twice in the same place. Even Dale the Bully praised me, saying it was a clever way to get a week off of school and still be well for the weekend. And I now knew the answer to Gabby's next inane question: "So, what did the pioneers do if they had to throw up?"

"Just lean over the side of the wagon and let 'er rip, Gabby. Just let 'er fly."

CHAPTER 17

"THE FINAL BOW"

The end was in sight. May was used not only for wrapping up our pioneer projects, but it was also for making sure the fifth graders went out in a blaze of glory. The way to achieve this lofty goal? Produce a school play. A real play. With a real script. Not some fanciful concoction like the ones we had put on in earlier grades, such as *Frosty the Snowman and Rudolph the Reindeer visit the Snow Queen*. This was a play with its roots in history and legend, a tale to excite any red-blooded American boy—*Robin Hood*.

I assumed that Mr. Paducci chose it because he liked boys and didn't care if the girls were upset that—other than Maid Marian—there were no glamorous parts for them. More likely it was his shrewd way to keep the boys, with their hyperactive-out-of-control-summer's-just-around-the-corner-so-let's-blow-up-the-school attitude, otherwise occupied.

As much as I loved sports, I also craved the theatre's spotlight. And there were some hard feelings from past years piled up like rejection slips. Because of my nondescript personality, I had been cast in second grade as an Elf with exactly one line: "All rise for the Snow Queen!"

In third grade, I played a traffic cop in a bicycle-safety-themed production. My one line in this dreary drama was: "Rule #4—always come to a complete stop at a stop sign." I almost blew that line when my mom took a picture from the first row as I began to speak, and the flashbulb nearly blinded me. Disoriented, I stumbled over the words.

Fourth grade, however, provided the ultimate insult. I came to tryouts prepared to blow the competition away and land a major role in a thrilling Arabian nights

133

production. But, the day before, I developed a case of laryngitis. Rasping, I whispered my lines in a barely audible croak. The two female directors, who were assistants to Mrs. Quantrell, held my illness against me in spite of my well-known "playground voice." Not even my rugged, Kirk Douglas looks could save me. Cast as "stage left spotlight," I spent the play hunched over out of sight in the darkened wings aiming a bright beam in the direction of the main characters. I was devastated. The bitterness of that slight had not left me a full year later, and I swore to get my revenge by earning one of the key roles.

I was optimistic. For one thing, Mr. Paducci, having overlooked the throwing-up-in-the-hallway incident, still liked me. For another, one of my good school friends, Tim Thompson, was chosen to be assistant director. A bright, earnest boy, Tim's only goal in life was to become an F.B.I. agent someday.

On the playground, he regaled us with lengthy narratives of the Feds and how they had brought to justice, one way or another, the nation's most wanted criminals: John Dillinger, Machine Gun Kelly, Baby Face Nelson. Tim had listened to me rattle off starting line-ups in a deep, resonant voice, and I was confident he had faith in my abilities.

The day before tryouts, I refused to speak all day. Resting my voice was crucial in order to avoid a repeat of last year's untimely disability. Before leaving for school on D-day, I soaked my throat with honey and lemon. I was asked to read for several lead parts, and—good news—I didn't blow it.

The next morning, we scrambled to the cast list, posted outside Mr. Paducci's classroom. Chris Branson, a blond-haired, charismatic boy, had been picked to play Robin Hood; Mark Von Better was to play his sidekick Little John; my old friends Doug and Ralph had been delegated the roles of Friar Tuck and Will Scarlett respectively; Barbara Zeitler, second grade's Snow Queen, hit pay dirt again as Maid Marian. That left me. For a gut-churning minute, fear assaulted my soul. I had been abandoned again, left without hope on the island of my banished dreams. And then, I saw it near the bottom of the list. I had been cast as the villain of all villains, that evil scoundrel the Sheriff of Nottingham. Oh, glory! Never again would I languish in the dim light of a bit part or squat in the dark out of the grasp of fame and fortune. I would finally and forever be what I had been made to be: an actor. Move over, Mr. Heston.

Rehearsals were held after school and, in the week preceding the performance, during school hours. Mr. Paducci stayed behind with the class while key cast members worked in the small, hot gymnasium under Tim's instruction. He turned out to be a stern, no-nonsense director, a role that he saw as a prelude to F.B.I. agent. He rooted out bad acting the way he would someday combat crime. If he saw it, he attacked it. "Chris, stand up straight and walk like a man! You're Robin Hood, the hero, remember?"

Apparently, Tim saw no contradiction in the fact that Robin Hood was actually an outlaw making war against an ancient agent of the law. I mentioned this to him once, and he told me that, unless I wanted to be handing out programs at the door, I should shut up and do what he told me.

But he blocked scenes well. In a scene where my soldiers and I pursued the fleeing bandit to an abandoned cabin, we entered to find an old woman knitting in a rocking chair (Robin Hood in disguise). Tim instructed me to walk up to the woman with my men behind me in single file. When I held up my hand to signal them to halt, the first of the four was to stop short, causing the other three to crash into him from behind. This sophisticated physical comedy was perfectly placed to add levity in order to break the tension of the scene. It also enhanced the bumbling characterization of the Sheriff's soldiers. No doubt about it. Tim had a bright future leading fellow agents into machine gun fire.

The costumes, however, were the icing on the cake. Created by an assembly line of moms, they were the most elaborate elementary school costumes ever seen. Mine consisted of a red pullover, black pants, and black boots. Covering all of the shirt except the sleeves was a shiny silver jacket made of tin foil. A similar helmet and sword completed the outfit. Glued onto my face were a black mustache and goatee. Staring at the evil image in the mirror, I was transported to Thespian heaven.

The night of the play was probably like any other opening in the history of the theatre. Costumes were donned and make-up was applied to the background sound of flushing toilets as diarrhea assailed our nerve-wracked systems. Proud parents, squeezed onto mini-chairs, were scrunched together like misshapen globs of Silly Putty, melting in the ninety-five degree heat and jungle-like humidity. Their voices buzzed loudly in anticipation. Would this be the beginning, they dared to wonder, of their child prodigy's rapid ascent up the ladder of stardom? Would their daughter be the next Annette Funicello or Hayley Mills? Would their son be the next Beaver Cleaver?

Believe it or not, the show went off without a hitch. The carefully choreographed sword fight between Robin and the Sheriff at the play's climax put accomplished fencers to shame. A minor mishap did occur, however, when I struck Robin's sword so hard with mine that both of our foil-encased cardboard weapons bent in half. The audience, on the edges of their seats with tension and leg cramps, didn't appear to notice. The applause at curtain call was deafening, our parents' shadowy, smiling faces shining with sweat.

Backstage, warm embraces abounded. We had done it, and we were plump with pride. Bound together for six years, it was our last group achievement. Many of us were being sent off to separate junior highs and would drift apart as friends often do. None of us would ever be Hollywood actors, although Tim would eventually achieve his dream of becoming an F.B.I. agent. But for now, hugging-jumping-shouting-praising as we stuffed our mouths with cupcakes and chugged down Hawaiian Punch, one thing was real. Fifth graders ruled the world!

The day before the last day of school, a sacred tradition was upheld. The six male employees of the school—Mr. Paducci (fifth grade), Mr. Somers (fifth grade), Mr. Beeton (fourth grade), Mr. Harmon (principal), Mr. Smith (custodian), and Mr. Stanley (bookkeeper)—challenged the fifth grade boys to a "World Championship" softball game. Since this was light years before Title IX, girls were not allowed to play. Truth be told, they didn't want to. They much preferred to stand and cheer loudly for the men to beat the living snot out of the jerky boys who had tormented them throughout K-5. We were up against it big time.

Two jocks, Mark Von Better and "Yogi" Yablonsky, were team co-captains. They were assigned the task of arranging a line-up and positions for all the fifth grade boys. The goal was that each boy would play at least two of the seven innings in the field. Luck would determine whether he got an at-bat during his playing tenure. The day before the big game, I checked out the list, again posted in the upstairs hallway near Mr. Paducci's classroom.

What the blazes? Sixth and seventh inning catcher? I hated catcher. Catcher was the most dangerous position on the field. Why, only last year at recess, I had witnessed Artie Burghoff take an errant bat to the face. Blood spurted out like Niagara Falls as a clearly dazed Artie spun in circles screaming for help. The jagged scar remained a grim reminder of the day he had played catcher. Would this—or something worse—be my fate? Catchers were routinely hit with foul tips in the face, chest, knees, and groin. They were bowled over on close plays at home and ran into metal backstops chasing foul balls while looking skyward. Furthermore, the girls would pay no attention to me. Hunched over like a gnome behind the plate, the catcher represented the least glamorous player on the team. While the shortstop was making backhanded fielding gems on hard-hit grounders, and the outfielders were diving for line drives in the gaps, the catcher was squatting awkwardly and chanting phrases like: "Hey, batta-batta, swing!" or "One thing is without a doubt, pitcher's gonna strike you out!"

Besides this ignominy, I wasn't even in the game until the next-to-last inning. I found out that, with this year's fast, hard-hitting team, the game plan was to get ahead in the early innings with the best players and hang on for victory. In other words, I was a we-have-to-put-you-in-the-game-so-we'll-hide-you-at-catcher-just-don't-make-any-mistakes-and-blow-it-for-us substitute, aka scrub. Charlie Brown never had it so bad.

Game day broke sunny. But by the noon starting time, the sky was overcast. The game was, as predicted, high-scoring. Dale the Bully, who looked old enough to be an adult, played all-time catcher for the teachers. We heard his parents cut a deal with the principal so he could move up with the rest of us, and this was a major part of the accord. But with pitcher and only five other position players, they were still an infielder and an outfielder short. Nonetheless, they seemed to be good athletes and were giving us a game, with the score 12-10 in our favor at the end of four innings.

As the top of the fifth began, so did the rain. The drops fell lightly at first, then more steadily as the teachers mounted a rally. A two-out, bases-loaded triple by Mr. Paducci put them in front 13-12. And then the skies opened. The crowd sprinted for shelter, followed by the teachers; finally, the forlorn fifth graders came in from the downpour. Entering the building, I saw Gabby Gustoson hanging onto a rain-soaked Mr. Paducci, gazing into his face with primordial lust and unabashed hero worship mixed into one.

Breaking away from him, Gabby approached me. "Ha. Ha," she smirked. "You lost."

"Did not," I countered.

"Did too. By one run." Someone must have told her this. She wasn't bright enough to have figured it out for herself.

"Did not," I repeated. "We didn't get our ups in the bottom of the fifth. That means the teachers' runs in the top of the fifth don't count. We won, 12-10."

The bemused look on her face told me that she had absolutely no clue what I was talking about. It was as if I had tried to explain tagging up at third on a fly out or the infield fly rule to her. It was a debate that had no common ground.

"Say what you want, but the teachers won." She smiled and then added with malice, "And you didn't even play."

She was right. The storm had erased any chance I might have had to get into the close contest and become the unexpected hero. But in my tormented mind, I heard the way it would be told in years to come, passed down through generations of kids eager to earn the spotlight for themselves.

"And then, with the bases loaded, two out, and the fifth graders clinging to a one-run lead in the final inning, Mr. Paducci let the bat slip while swinging and popped it up behind home plate. The bat struck the catcher full in the face, breaking his nose and knocking out his two front teeth. Bewildered, with blood streaming from his nostrils, the brave ball player staggered toward the backstop and pinned the ball up against it with his glove. His dramatic catch surely saved the day. And remember, he was a scrub."

"What was his name?" they would ask in awe, eyes wide and mouths agape.

"Why, it's over here in the glass case, engraved on the annual MVP trophy."

And thus I would pass into legend, as we all would. In fact, every fifth grader in the world would have his or her own memory book to carry as he or she moved along in life. It would be crammed with embellished stories and half-truths from an ancient time—a time when kids ruled the playgrounds, teachers ruled the classrooms, and Howdy Doody ruled the airwaves.

PART IV
VACATION

CHAPTER 18

"WESTWARD HO!"

On the last day of school, we received our grades for our projects. In spite of my attractive cover art, a Venus Paradise color-by-number portrait of an American Indian chief, I earned a "C." Whatever happened to rewarding creative artistic expression? Gabby also got a "C" and promptly "broke up" with Mr. Paducci. One nugget I gained from the project was that it took the rugged pioneers six months to traverse the country from Illinois to their land of milk and honey, California. When my father announced that we would be taking a vacation there, I was shocked to learn we would make the same trip in less than a week.

This was to be our first-ever genuine vacation. Three years earlier, we had gone north to the Wisconsin Dells and stayed for three days. This was decades before the Dells were turned into the world's largest man-made water park, although some commercialism had crept in. We thrilled at a steam engine train ride through the woods, boat tours of the Lower and Upper Dells, the Stand Rock Indian Ceremonial, the Tommy Bartlett Water Show, Story Book Gardens, Biblical Gardens, and the amphibious Ducks. That this—or any other—world existed outside of our quaint suburban enclave was a wondrous discovery, and our upcoming trip westward found us half-crazed with anticipation.

One fact was certain: we would not be alone. Millions of Americans, spurred on by Dinah Shore's melodic plea to "See the U.S.A. in your Chevrolet," were taking to the country's highways like never before. Popular destinations included: Niagara Falls, Gettysburg, and Washington, D.C., to the east, and Mount Rushmore, Yellowstone National Park, and the Grand Canyon to the west. California, however, had recently experienced another Gold

Rush of sorts, thanks largely to the creation of America's first themed amusement park. Opened on July 17, 1955, in Anaheim, a country suburb of Los Angeles, it was named Disneyland after its creator.

Ronald Reagan teamed with co-hosts Bob Cummings and Art Linkletter for the park's grand opening, which was televised by ABC-TV. The fledgling network had invested heavily in the park and was anxious to turn a profit. During the late 1950s, Walt Disney used his Sunday night TV show to lure families to bite the financial bullet and drive across the country from places as far away as New York and Florida to experience imagination working overtime.

During the park's first five years, every new ride or attraction was given the royal treatment, a "special" spot during Disney's show. Also, the newest additions—the Matterhorn Bobsleds, the Submarine Voyage, and the Monorail—were christened by then vice-president Richard Nixon, a native Californian. So, years before the Clark Griswold family made its pilgrimage to Wally World, we set off to see the Rocky Mountains, the Grand Canyon, Hoover Dam, and Disney's magical park.

"Are we there yet?"

"Not yet," my mother patiently answered from her front seat navigator's post.

Tommy, Linda, and I were crammed in the back seat of the non-air conditioned Buick LeSabre, surrounded by books to read or color, cheap car games to play, and a mound of sugary snacks such as Hostess Cupcakes and Twinkies to curb our perpetual hunger. We weren't out of Illinois yet.

"Why don't we play a game?" Mom suggested. In those days, moms were the game show hosts of family vacations. Their imaginations were essential in keeping the peace among the tired travelers so the dads could focus on eating up the endless miles. In fact, dads didn't speak unless absolutely necessary, seldom a cheerful event.

Almost all car games had something to do with looking frantically out the windows to find an object or building—"Let's see who's first to spot a bus or truck or dog or farm or gas station" or whatever. A variation of this was to *count* something—"Let's count the buses or trucks or dogs or farms or gas stations" or whatever. This was, of course, a sure-fire method of increasing tension, quickly leading to open hostilities.

"I saw a dog!"

"Where?"

"Back there! In the field!"

"Did not!"

"Did too!"

"Oh, yeah? Well, I saw two dogs back in the town we just went through!"

"What? That's not fair! You have to say 'em when you see 'em!"

"Do not!"

"Do too! Mom, he's changin' the rules!"

"Liar!"

"Cheat!"

This crescendo ceased suddenly upon hearing Dad's voice, seemingly from afar, which always surprised us because we had forgotten he was there. "That's enough! I swear, if I have to stop this car and come back there . . ."

But these spot-'em, call-'em-out games were trivial in my mom's mind. She expected us to engage in games that required us to use critical thinking skills. Her favorite car game began, "My mother sent me to the grocery store to find something that begins with the letter _____." Assuming she didn't pick "X," we were required to stretch our brains and come up with whatever she was thinking. Most letters had multiple possibilities, causing the game to last for hours, an effective strategy in the battle for harmony on the highway.

"Corn . . . Cabbage . . . Cucumbers . . . Cereal . . . Candy . . . Crackers . . . Cottage Cheese . . ."

"Nope . . . Nope."

"Ketchup!"

"That's a 'K,' you fool!"

"There's nothing left!" someone ultimately yelled in exasperation.

"Think harder," Mom-the-encourager teased.

"I can't! My brain's on fire!"

Finally, a lucky guess. "Cantaloupe!"

"Right!" Mom smiled.

"Boy, that was a tough one!"

"My turn!" yelled the winner as the car cruised swiftly past the cornfields.

The first couple of days were an endless whirl of motion, mile after mile of gray ribbon disappearing rapidly beneath the Buick. Neon signs beckoned us to pull into the gravel parking lots of cheap motels when the setting sun scorched our tired eyes. On the third day, our first sight of the Rocky Mountains told us we weren't in Kansas anymore. We first thought that they were a gathering of clouds. But each successive mile brought them into sharper focus as they shaped themselves into a massive wall of tree-covered rock that, I thought, must have scared the crap out of the pioneers—or at least their horses.

Gradually engulfed by the mountains, we fell silent. This was beyond our realm of experience, and the awesome setting put us into a state of reverence.

"God made all this," Mom reminded her children.

"What's that on the ground?" Tommy asked.

"I think it's snow!" I shouted.

"It is," said Dad.

"In June?"

Dad pulled the car to the side of the winding road, and we piled out. Cold air smacked our faces.

"Holy sh - - - shoot!" I cried out. "It really is snow!" This was too much. Snow. In the middle of summer.

"Owww!" Tommy's snowball had hit its mark, my back.

The battle commenced. As the five of us—Linda in Dad's spare arm—scooped up snow and pelted one another, a car with a Colorado license plate drove by, slowed down momentarily, and quickly sped ahead. "Tourists" most likely came to their minds.

And tourists we were. Dad proudly proved it to the world by stopping at every roadside "historical marker" and lining us up alongside it for a family snapshot. These pictures inevitably showed someone in a cranky mood, a haggard face pouting into the bright sunshine. Tommy earned infamy for these expressions of despair, usually accompanied by a balled fist rubbing a bleary eye to emphasize that he'd been rudely awakened from a nap. And who could blame him?

We were wide-awake, however, when we reached our next destination, the Grand Canyon. Standing at the guardrails, we watched Dad click off about sixty-eight frames, capturing its beauty with as much success as placing a butterfly in a jar. Then, without warning, he turned to us and calmly said, "I want a good picture of you kids with the Grand Canyon in the background. So, you guys step over the rail, and I'll hand your sister to you."

Hello? Did my father just say to us, "Dear children of mine. I've decided to murder you all and make it look like an accident. While the authorities search for your bodies, your mother and I will continue on to Disneyland."

"C'mon, move it, before other people come around and spoil the shot."

Or possibly, I thought, before the park ranger comes around, sees how you're mistreating your children, and arrests you on the spot.

"C'mon, guys, I'm waiting."

Protect us, Jesus, I prayed as I climbed cautiously over the railing and stepped down on the other side. Tommy, ever eager for adventure, followed.

"Hank," my mom said, "do you think they'll be safe?"

"Sure. Mikey will watch over them."

Oh, nice. Place the burden of keeping younger siblings from taking one step too far and plunging off a cliff on the shoulders of an eleven-year-old boy.

Linda was raised over the bright yellow railing— "Look, Dad, a caution color"—and handed off to us. We inched our way along the narrow ledge of red rock. Peeking over the precipice, I saw the silver shine from the river below.

"That's far enough!" Dad barked.

Are you sure? Maybe we could balance on the edge if it made for a better picture. We slowly turned around, our backs facing outer space.

"Smile!"

My dad's "best vacation picture ever" shows three terrified kids huddled together, sickening smiles spread across their quivering lips, fingers intertwined in vise-like grips, legs bent uncertainly at the knees, and tufts of hair blown sideways. Behind them, the Grand Canyon yawns upward, poised to swallow them whole. Rumor has it they have never fully recovered. The oldest one's body still twitches spasmodically from time to time.

Our trek across the desert redefined phrases such as: "I need a drink of water"; "My shirt is sticking to me"; and "Damn, it's hot out!" Tommy, the only smart one in the group, became instantly popular with his army canteen. Wrapped in faded green cloth, the metallic container was refilled with cold water at every gas station stop. As the scorching wind beat on us through the open windows, we bartered with Tinhorn Tommy for a sip of the life-saving liquid. Even Dad, the back of his shirt soaked with sweat, let the swindler sit on his lap and "drive" the car—were there no "Rules of the Road" back then?—in exchange for a swig of the icy elixir. I gave in and swapped him a "Tom and Jerry" comic book for a drink. The only problem—besides Tommy's shouts of "That's enough!" after the first drop reached my parched throat—was that, ten minutes out of a station, the water was already tepid. A half hour out, it was like drinking from the hot water faucet.

The nadir of our vacation was the one hundred and four degree day at Hoover Dam. Heat encircled our exhausted bodies as we stood on the black asphalt for the photo shoot. Bravely facing the merciless sun, we smiled weakly, Linda's face a vermillion hue. The thought crept into my weary mind that this was it. Like the courageous pioneers, we had weathered the harsh elements and the wagon master's brutal sunrise-to-sunset schedule. Driven like pack mules, we had given all we had. Now, here in the desert, we were doomed to die a painful, agonizing death with thoughts of the Promised Land—Disneyland—foremost on our fatigued minds. I shut my eyes tightly so as not to witness the vultures gathering overhead. My strength abandoned me. I began to fade . . . fade . . . fade . . .

"Mikey, open your damn eyes and stand up straight!" The wagon master, always the last to concede defeat, spoke sharply, snapping me back to brutal reality.

We were to go on then, though there be mountains and deserts and hostile savages, the latter disguised as commercially licensed owners of blood-sucking tourist traps. We would show our ancestors that their trail-blazing efforts had not been in vain. We would carve our own legacy of freedom and adventure.

Soon thereafter, we stood on the shores of the mighty Pacific Ocean, its majestic waves crashing onto our soaked sneakers, and proudly faced the western sun as it dropped rapidly from the sky. It was then that we realized, instinctively, that the trip had been worth it just to watch the sun set beneath the water's curtain. My father's camera hung motionless at his side.

CHAPTER 19

"WHEN YOU WISH UPON A STAR"

The Pirates of the Caribbean, The Haunted Mansion, It's a Small World, Space Mountain, Splash Mountain, and Big Thunder Mountain Railroad. These were just some of the attractions that weren't even seedlings in the imaginative soil of Walt Disney's mind when my family first hit Disneyland. But, trust me, there was still plenty to see, including the Matterhorn Mountain, visible as we approached the park. Tommy, never the bright one, pointed at it out the car window and yelled, "What the hell is that?"

My father immediately swerved to the side of Harbor Boulevard, stopped the car, and reached back with his bear-like paw to give him a few whacks. For the rest of the short drive to check into the motel, Tommy sniffed in mock sorrow over his deserved punishment. Dad's reaction was simple. "Be quiet back there, or I'll give you something to cry about!"

The motel was like nothing we'd ever seen on our cross-country excursion. Called the Space Age Lodge, it had a Tomorrowland theme, with multi-colored planets and asteroids everywhere. Cheesy beyond belief, yet the coolest place we had ever stayed. And the most incredible part was the view from the second floor balcony across the parking lot. There it sat, "The Happiest Place on Earth," within our grasp. However, because we had arrived late in the afternoon, we were not to visit the park until the next day.

"Don't worry," Mom smiled. "We'll be at the park tomorrow."

Yeah, I thought, kinda like the Titanic passengers were told they'd be in New York "tomorrow."

No use arguing. We contented ourselves by wandering around the Topiary Gardens, which featured cleverly crafted models of Mickey, Donald, Goofy, Pluto, and other Disney characters shaped out of living evergreens. This thrilled us for about two and a half minutes, and then we left for dinner.

Walking down the noisy, cluttered avenue, we noticed the many businesses, already closing in like sharks on Disney's suburban utopia, beckoning to us. We came upon a Sambo's restaurant. A famous pancake house, it supposedly derived its name from a colorful children's book. The mascot, a forerunner, I suppose, to Ronald McDonald, was a stereotyped Negro boy whose image was unceremoniously plastered on the menus and placemats. In the days just before the Civil Rights Movement gained momentum, Sambo's white smile and bulging eyes were viewed as comical, a way to keep children amused as they downed hot stacks of pancakes smothered in fruit and whipped cream. Sorry, Sambo, we didn't know any better.

That night, we stood on our balcony and watched the fireworks explode over Disneyland. The next morning, we took the shuttle bus to the front gate, Mickey-in-flowers greeting us as we stepped off. Was this Heaven?

Dad purchased the tickets. Mom cornered us. "Now, listen. You boys help keep an eye on Linda. And if you get lost, look out for one of us in the crowd."

This would not be difficult. Mom was dressed in a bright pink blouse with white tennis shorts; Dad was wearing a patterned shirt covered with lions, elephants, and giraffes. Perhaps he could fill in for the Jungle Cruise guides later in the day.

"The man explained the ticket books to me," Dad said as he came over to where we were standing. For that's what they were, books of tickets labeled A through E. The A ones, ironically, were the cheapest. One example was a walk through Sleeping Beauty's Castle, not much above a county fair haunted house. Here, visitors witnessed a few scenes from the film that culminated in viewing Sleeping Beauty . . . well, sleeping. The E ones were mostly the big attractions. Suspiciously, there were never quite enough of these to ride all the cool rides. But, look! Ticket booths in convenient locations throughout the park where a cash-strapped family could buy more and just skip dinner.

Midday, the bright blue California sky above us. A raft to Tom Sawyer's Island, a paradise for boys. Running on ahead, Tommy and I were free to follow winding trails, climb rock formations, poke through spooky caves, traverse suspension bridges, and fire fake rifles from the towers of an old fort.

"Mike, have you ever seen such a place?"

"No, never." I shot at an invisible Indian.

"What if we had Johnny and the other guys here?"

"I know. We could play all day."

Zigzagging back in the direction of the dock, we caught a glimpse of Mom and Dad trying to guide Linda—one petrified step after another—across the giant, swaying bridge. She was crying loudly. They were heading for the fort.

"They'll be busy for awhile. Let's keep going," I suggested, "and see what's at the other end of the island."

"Okay."

An old abandoned mill, water dripping casually over its revolving wheel, sat surrounded by tall marsh grass. A red-haired, freckle-faced boy wearing an oversized straw hat stepped suddenly out of the scenery.

"Howdy!"

"Hi," I timidly returned his greeting; Tommy slid behind me. "Who are you?"

"Who am I? Why, I'm none other than Tom Sawyer. I live on this here island."

"*The* Tom Sawyer?"

"Ain't but one, I reckon."

"Well, if you live here, what do you do all day?"

"Whatever I like. My friend Huck Finn sneaks away from his pappy, and together we hunt and fish. But mostly we just play pirates. Would you boys like to join us?"

If I'd been old enough to have an orgasm, I would have. "Heck, yes! What do we do?"

"Follow me. We'll go meet up with ole Huck, and if he ain't contrary toward you, we'll swear you into our club with a blood oath."

"What's that?" squealed Tommy.

"Shut up," I said. "Don't matter. We can take it. Lead the way."

And Tom Sawyer did just that; he took us for the ride of our lives. We tried to keep up as best as we could, but we lost him in Injun Joe's lair. There we were, two Chicago toughs lost in the dark-as-damnation cave, near to peeing our pants from listening to the mournful wails of Joe's ghost.

A pair of giant hands seized us by the shoulders. "Where have you monkeys been?"

"Dad!"

On the raft trip back to the mainland, Tommy and I babbled about our discovery and pleaded to be allowed to stay and take the blood oath. Well, I did anyway. Tommy wanted nothing more to do with Sawyer and Finn and their shenanigans. He felt fortunate to have escaped alive.

Downtrodden, I stepped onto dry land and, family in tow, made my way toward less adventurous destinations. However, I glanced back once more at the island just to see if . . . and there he was. Blue jeans. Bare feet. Palaverin' with a couple more boys. Then, as if he sensed my gaze across the Rivers of America, Tom Sawyer turned and looked at me. A big catfish-eatin' grin spread slyly over his sunburned face, and he raised his hand and waved at me. POW! I'd been had.

He wasn't Tom Sawyer. He was a Disney shill. He was part of the act. He'd left my brother and me behind to be murdered in Injun Joe's cave, and he thought it was funny. Tom Sawyer, my ass. Why, his real name was probably Corky McPumpkin, and he was sixteen years old and took Annette out on weekends and felt her up. How could I have been so stupid, so utterly naïve, as to believe he lived on the island? Pirates? I'll give him pirates.

In the end, I realized that I had only been tricked by my own vivid imagination, and that was precisely why Disneyland existed in the first place. The magic kingdom allowed young and old alike to cast aside the realities of everyday life and dream of something better—or at least more fun. I believed because I wanted to believe. Nothing more, nothing less. And though I still bristled at the thought of Mr. Sawyer's weekend indiscretions, I forgave him.

Disney after dark. One couldn't see the dips and curves inside the darkened Matterhorn, a prelude to Space Mountain years later. The Jungle Cruise, its animals lit with tinted spotlights as the boat slid through murky waters, was surreal. And the fireworks, viewed from the upper deck of the Mark Twain steamboat, were colorful and grand.

As we departed the paddle wheeler, my dad's ear caught the sweet sounds of a jazz band and followed them to an outdoor café. We bought soft drinks and sat down at a round table near the rear of the half-filled restaurant.

"This is beautiful," Dad said, his eyes fixed on the stage.

Mom agreed.

Tommy and I, bored, finished our drinks quickly, hoping to compel our music-mad parents to move along.

When the man passed in front of us, we hardly gave him a second glance. He was wearing a navy blue blazer and tie. His most unusual feature was his moustache—very few men wore them in this post-War era. Unexplainably, I was suddenly drawn to watching him. He took a seat at an empty table near ours and made himself comfortable, lighting a cigar while he watched the band. His eyes sparkled with delight, like a father observing his children, and his smile was a kind one.

"That's him, you know," my mom whispered in my ear.

"Who?" For a hot moment, I thought it might have been Tom Sawyer in disguise, just starting his sordid nighttime rounds.

"Walt Disney." Her voice was shaking when she spoke. And why shouldn't it? Here was the man who had provided her children with marvelous, quality TV. The man who had given her a reason to take her precious darlings to movie theatres to see classic animated films. So what if the youngsters had trouble getting to sleep at night thinking about Snow White lost in the forest, Pinocchio locked in a cage, and Bambi's mother lying dead on a frozen field? Here was a genuine American original, an icon to millions—and he sat a mere two tables over.

"Get up," said Mom. The command startled me. "Go see him."

"What?"

"You heard me. Go talk to him."

"What? Why me?"

"Because you're the oldest."

Technically, of course, this wasn't true. I glanced at my father, whose head bobbed up and down in time to the beat. He didn't have a clue.

"I mean it," she said, flashing me her sternest look. "I want you to shake his hand."

Oh, Lord, I thought, she's finally cracked. "Why? What'll I say to him?"

"Tell him your name. And tell him you watch his show every Sunday night."

"What if he won't talk to me?"

"Of course he'll talk to you. He's Walt Disney."

And that was that. I rose, looking at Tommy for encouragement. He was asleep, his face resting comfortably in a puddle of drool on the table. I moved timidly across the café and stood silently next to the great man. I cleared my throat, and he looked up at me and smiled.

"Hello, son. What can I do for you?"

This was unbelievable. I was hearing the same Uncle Walt voice that had introduced countless adventures and fantasies to families huddled around their TVs across America.

I stuck out my sweat-soaked palm. "Hello, Mr. Disney. My name is Mike."

"Well, hello, Mike, is that your family over there?"

My mother waved with both hands. My father, now aware, fumbled for his camera. Linda had awakened Tommy, and they both stared trance-like at Walt and me.

Embarrassed, I nodded.

"Where are you from?"

"Chicago."

"Is that so? Did you know that I was born in Chicago?"

No, I thought, but I know that you brought Annette into my life, and for that alone I'd be willing to bow down before you in front of all these people. Instead, I answered politely, "No, sir."

"Are you enjoying yourself at the park?"

"Yes, sir."

"Well, I'm glad. Why don't you head on back to your folks now? Thanks for stopping by to visit."

If I could have foreseen the next five seconds, I would have tarried longer. For as soon as I walked out of the scene, Dad's camera lens clicked. Simply put, it was the finest photo my father ever took. After years of cutting off people's heads or moving his hands and blurring the picture, he finally got it right. The picture clearly framed Walt Disney's profile, cigar poised in right hand, gazing serenely at his beloved Firehouse Five Plus Two, a band made up of some of his closest friends and animators. Perhaps it was for the best. It was, I think, enough that I met him, talked to him, one-on-one. And, five years later, when the world mourned his untimely death, I knew it had been.

CHAPTER 20

"ALL ABOARD!"

The train chugged slowly out of the Disneyland station. I loved trains. The Chicago-Northwestern line ran only a block from our house. At four, I had been lured by its sound so much that I'd bounded up the street, fat little legs churning, to watch its sleek body glide by. A year later, perhaps to keep me from running away, my father built a Lionel train layout in our basement. Lower and upper tracks circled past towns, farmhouses, utility poles, and billboards touting Sinclair gasoline, Winston cigarettes, and Maytag washers and dryers. The "surprise" for the first time observer was watching in suspended horror as the Santa Fe sped toward the far wall with seemingly nowhere to go. At the last second, it dove into a mountain tunnel and out of sight—back into my dad's work section—only to re-emerge five seconds later from another tunnel passage. Hours were spent running the variety of engines and cars that my dad continued to collect, and at Christmas the little village was covered in "snow."

The train picked up speed. I had wanted to ride the Disneyland Railroad around the park's perimeter one more time before leaving, and my parents had acquiesced. I was seated on the inside of the long bench seats, the ideal spot to look out upon Disney's empire and reflect on the themed landscapes. That train ride found me on the threshold of a new life, with a new school and new friends waiting just around the bend. My childhood was falling behind me as the steam engine swallowed up track.

The train rattled past a wall of jungle plants, the borders of Adventureland. Sure, African animals and native headhunters were thrilling, but could they really compare with the terrors of the playground or the excitement of the ball diamond? Was steering a boat through the muddy waters of the Congo more exhilarating than the freedom of riding a bike "no hands" down a sloping suburban street at ever-increasing speed? Hardly. And as fierce as painted warriors with poisonous blowguns rising suddenly out of secret hiding places might seem, I'd rather face a hundred blood-thirsty tribes than the "I'll see you at recess" glare of Dale the Bully. The playground, like an African veldt, was a communal waterhole, where survival of the fittest dictated the human food chain.

Adventureland? Ha! Adventure was sorting through Bobby's stack of doubles looking for a Banks, Santo, Musial, or Clemente. It was building a tree house in Johnny's back yard or stockpiling snowballs within the walls of a carefully constructed snow fort. It was placing pennies on the red-hot rails of the train tracks on a steamy hot day or catching fireflies in an old fruit jar as darkness settled on a warm summer's eve. It was life, and so far it outdistanced Disney's imaginary jungle by a million miles.

The train broke into the clear, moonlit landscape of Frontierland. The greatest portion of our 1950s childhood had been devoted to playing, watching, and reading about Cowboys and Indians. Prime time TV featured nightly gunfights as Matt Dillon, Wyatt Earp, and a host of heroes attempted to bring law and order to the Old West. These half hour story lines presented clear-cut good guys and bad guys. And like these TV Westerns, the "We Like Ike" decade we had grown up in had no moral ambiguities. There was good and evil in the world, and the sooner we understood this, the better our lives would be.

But the world, like my life, was changing. We had recently been told of a "New Frontier," and the next decade would prove to be so. The nineteenth century pioneers had once grappled with the concepts of Texas independence, a wagon trail to the Pacific, and a railroad that would link two coasts. Our frontier would include an un-popular war to stop the spread of Communism, a soul-searching reappraisal of the civil rights of Black Americans, and the fathomless conquering of outer space.

The train shot out of the past and into the realm of Fantasyland, the lighted towers of the castle shining brilliantly over the kingdom. It was the most popular "land" in the park for kids. And why not? Rides such as Snow White, Alice in Wonderland, Peter Pan, and Mr. Toad gave children a brief respite from reality. Even I, a hardened eleven-year-old boy, marveled at the beauty of sprawling London twinkling beneath Peter's magic ship as it took flight toward Neverland. But what of my real life fantasies?

It probably goes without saying that I dreamed of playing in the Major Leagues. It would happen like this. The weary old scout, bedraggled from endless days on the road, would stop by a Little League game and marvel at the Italian kid at third with the smooth glove and rocket arm who had five hits and eight RBIs. The boy's father would sign a contract on the spot, bonus included, and a future star would be born. When "Mighty Mike," as the fans would dub him, finally reached the "show" at seventeen, he would lead the Cubs to their first championship since the Dark Ages. Yeah, I laughed to myself as I saw the Dumbo ride in the distance—when elephants fly.

My other fantasy was to someday marry a beautiful girl. This was trickier now than it had once been. Before this summer, I fantasized about Mary Linder to the exclusion of all others. It was her soft, blond hair I yearned to stroke, her radiant lips I longed to kiss. But in the fall, although she lived but five blocks away, we would be bussed to different junior high schools. In the real world, this was equivalent to being shipped off to different continents. For all practical purposes, it was out-of-sight, out-of-mind. Bobby's sister Cyndi was now taking up more of my rapturous thoughts. This enchanted beauty was beginning to haunt my dreams in a way that made finding a Mickey Mantle in a new pack of Topps seem like kids' stuff. When I sent Bobby a postcard of the Grand Canyon, I had the impudence to add the P.S., "Say hi to Cyndi for me." Clearly, these were uncharted waters, and I had left my life jacket on the dock.

The train moved steadily toward Tomorrowland. One of this land's major attractions was "A Trip to the Moon," which would one day be updated to "A Trip to Mars" to keep it futuristic. Time moves fast like that. Nothing ever stays the same. It was a very scary thought, the future. I was not sure that—if someone told me it was possible to do so—I would want to see what my future held. I guessed it would be more or less of the same, the highs and lows of life that give it flavor. I figured I'd basically be happy even if I didn't marry Cyndi or play third base for the Cubs. Whatever was in store for me would happen as surely as the train would reach its destination, the Main Street station, where the trip had begun.

The train stammered to a stop. The conductor's voice crackled through the hidden speaker: "Ladies and gentlemen, boys and girls, this is the end of the line. The Disneyland Railroad is shuttin' down for the night. Hope you had a great day in the park. Come back and visit us soon. So long, folks!"

As we worked our way from the platform down the stairs, I glanced out at Main Street, U.S.A., the heart of a small Midwestern town. It was supposedly a replica of Marceline, Missouri, where Disney had spent many carefree childhood days. In my mind, I saw a tree-lined street too, where a row of neatly kept houses and lawns stretched out under a cloudless blue sky. Boys carrying bats, balls, and gloves steered bikes toward the field at the end of the block. Legs pumping, laughing in anticipation of the day ahead, they rode swiftly away from me until their figures blended into the horizon and disappeared from my sight.

9 781609 111212